MW00935650

TEETH

Also by Kelli Owen

TEETH

Kelli Owen

Gypsy Press

For the children of the night,
and the music they make.

Acknowledgements: Thank you to my wonderful daughter Amanda for listening to me rant for hours on end while I worked through various plot lines, themes, details, and dead ends. To my pre-readers of doom: Ron Dickie, Tod Clark, Dave Thomas, and Amy Vause. To Bob Ford, and his mother, since it's mostly their fault this particular monster was chosen—still waiting for your werewolves. To the friends and followers who volunteered their names. And of course, thanks Bram.

"We gladly feast on those who would subdue us."
~ *Addams Family* credo

"The world seems full of good men,
even if there are monsters in it."
~ Bram Stoker, *Dracula*

PROLOGUE

The tall, skinny man sat and flipped his armchair lever in a smooth, practiced motion—the footrest slamming upward to meet his feet. He pushed the button on the remote, and the television came *blaring* to life—the volume unexplainable in the otherwise quiet house. He reached up and gathered his shoulder-length hair into a low pony, expertly hooking the rubber band from his wrist around the loose strands.

A dog barked several houses over—a quick yip to greet a wandering cat, or an awareness of *his* presence. The couple across the street could be heard talking in excited tones through their open windows, whether they were arguing or naturally loud was unclear. The figure blocked out them *and* the dog, along with the distant sounds of sparse traffic on Main Street.

Looking through a gap in the curtains partially covering the window of the back door, he watched the skinny man's actions. The long narrow home made it easy to survey the layout, and was partially why it was chosen. The inside was as desolate and depressing as the neighborhood around it. The walls were bare of portraits, the garbage was full of empty tequila bottles and paper plates, and the table was stacked with job applications and unemployment stubs. He had no family, no friends, no job, no life. He had no business left unfinished.

No one will miss this one.

The man reached into the crumpled McDonald's bag and pulled a Big Mac free. The peace symbol tattooed on his inner wrist was briefly visible and completed the hippie persona the figure had perceived. The man expertly flicked the top of the cardboard container open, as canned laughter from the television faded into a commercial for Andy's Auto, the local car dealership. He lifted the burger's bun and pulled two pickles free, apparently believing it was easier to remove them than to request a special order.

As the television switched over to an obnoxiously loud commercial for *American Idol*, the figure opened the back door. The telltale creak a tenant may recognize was easily overpowered by the bad vocals in the living room.

The figure loved small-town mentality and wondered how long it would be before they began locking their doors, leaving outside lights on, and closing their curtains. Until then, he'd have free reign and he was going to enjoy it. Slipping into the house, he slinked across the cracked kitchen linoleum. The figure snuck up behind the man as he took the first bite from the heat lamp preserved sandwich.

The figure's motions sped up as he approached and he pierced the unsuspecting man's neck before the hippie had time to react. The man's eyes shot wide open as his blood poured from the wound in his jugular. The slickness squirted with an initial burst of pressure, pumped from a still-beating heart, before the fountain waned to a steady flow down the front of a dirty Dave Matthews t-shirt.

The figure quickly collected the spilling blood and watched the dying man with fascination.

Terror held the hippie motionless—his hand still in midair, but his sandwich fallen apart in his lap. His eyes widened as his fingers flicked briefly and moved sporadically, gesturing frantically toward his neck. Before he could wrap his hand around the wound or somehow apply enough pressure to stop the hemorrhaging, he began choking and spitting up flecks of blood.

He gasped and the figure knew whatever blood wasn't coming *out* of the wound was rushing toward the man's lungs. The man sputtered and seized briefly, before the will and fight faded in his eyes—much sooner than expected. Unblinking fear held is eyes open wide as their spark faded, and slowly the shine was replaced with a wordless matte plea. The man's lips were partially open, as if to speak, or robotically chew the bite still in his mouth.

A cruel smile spread across the figure's lips.

Vampires had stepped from the shadows almost fifty years ago and the world at large had renamed them, and welcomed them. Some wanted to *be* them. Others refused to accept them. After three decades of fear and confusion, a treaty was supposed to make everyone complacent neighbors—a new term for them, a clean slate for their history.

But technology gave voice to everyone with an Internet connection and social media caused havoc. Laws were suggested almost daily to *force* tolerance. Libel suits were being filed against historical belief and folklore. Prejudices were alive and well, and as real as the vampires. The *lamians*. The humans were torn between over-eager liberal acceptance and stoic intolerance bred by ignorance and fear. The *vampires* continued to claim they shouldn't be judged as a whole. It was upheaval and protests, banding together in song, and social warriors shaking fists at proclaimed indignities they'd chosen to fight for even though they weren't asked.

The figure found it all disgusting. *All* of it.

Vampires should have remained a secret. The humans should have remained afraid of the dark. And here, in the muddy waters of change, the figure knew he would wallow in their mistakes as he explored the taste of their deaths. He shut his eyes for a moment and inhaled deeply, enjoying the smell of blood as it washed over the room.

The life from victim number three succumbed as the slow trickle came to a stop, and the figure stood. He left the television on and the back door open. Stepping into the cool night air, he felt a chill on his skin where the blood had spattered. He whistled through his teeth, hoping to attract the barking dog. Let the animals feast on the meat he'd left behind. He had what he needed.

He'd taken the blood.

ONE

"Let's start with what you *think* you know?" Jacqueline took a sip of her coffee and put the cup down on the kitchen table. She folded her hands in motherly patience.

Tamara shrugged at the question. *I'm barely awake enough for school by eight o'clock, and Mom wants to have a serious conversation before seven?*

"I don't know. What I've seen on television or heard in school, I guess. You know they do a whole lamian awareness day every year, right? *Every. Year.*"

Jacqueline raised an eyebrow at her daughter's obstinate response.

"Sorry." Tamara knew the look and reworded her answer. "That Hollywood is wrong—mostly. And we're not *monsters*." She used air quotes on the word *monsters*, and sarcastically parroted information she'd been told too many times by too many teachers. "How about… we're a freaking living myth? Like unicorns." She smirked and put her hand to her forehead, sticking a finger out to represent the creature's horn. The glint in her hazel eyes was given extra shine as she stifled a yawn.

"They were—*We* were—*never* a myth." Jacqueline reached for a notebook Tamara hadn't even noticed, and slid it across the table, flipping it open as it slid to a stop between them. "Now come on, be serious."

"Fine. Sorry. I just didn't know we were doing this this morning." Tamara rubbed her eyes. "Whatcha got?"

"I've done a lot of research since your teeth came loose. Dad's side had nothing. His 23andMe finally came back and it showed absolutely *nothing*. Not even a trace. When *mine* came back… well, you know how that went down with your grandparents." She paused, a flash of anger washed across her expression.

Tamara knew the glare wasn't aimed at her, but rather the grandparents who'd been *un*invited to Christmas this year. Her mother's eyes, the same striking hazel as her own, seemed to drift off to something distant but returned in a blink and focused on Tamara.

"I'll never lie to you like they lied to me. I would never hide from you what you are. And we'll figure out *together* what that actually means. What *this* means."

"So, *your* tests… You're English, not Irish, and almost *full*-blood lamian?" Tamara had always loved her mother's naturally streaked hair—shiny brown with chunks of blonde, making it seem sun-kissed even in the dead of winter—but now she attributed those traits to her newfound bloodline, and Tamara was bummed about it. While she'd inherited her mother's *teeth*, she had her dad's bright red Irish hair. She usually put it in a perfectly planned messy bun, or a high pony, sometimes even double braids—anything to disguise it. Any style that would hide the fact it was the same long, lifeless red hair she had been teased for in elementary school when the older, meaner kids had referred to her as The Little *Drowning* Mermaid.

"Who finds out they're adopted after forty?" The sarcasm in the older woman's voice was *almost* playful, and Tamara knew she was mimicking her earlier snark. "Not telling me was bad enough, but then to find out the rest? The orthodontist? Braces I never needed. And then *surgery,* under the guise of *jaw* reconstruction, to remove my teeth before they could come in. Before the truth could come out. Can you even imagine?" Jacqueline gazed off into the distance for a moment, "I never thought their horrible close-minded attitude could be turned against me. Then again, I *thought* I was their child."

Tamara watched disgust and pain swirl in her mother's expression. She hated seeing her upset. "So do you *need* those pills then?" Tamara knew she'd be late for school if she didn't pull her mother back from the angry wallowing and get her on topic. She indicated the prescription bottle nestled among vitamins and headache medicine on the microwave.

"I guess I don't. I was never suffering from any rare *anemia*." Jacqueline shook her head and returned her attention to Tamara. "I mean, they worked for their true intentions. But from what I've gathered, I don't *need* a pill. I just have to adjust my diet. *Our* diet. I'll ask Dr. Hammond."

"Hammond?"

"Oh yeah. We won't be seeing the old family doctor or dentist anymore. Not after years of lying to me because they're old pals of my parents. We have a *new* doctor, and I've made an appointment for both of us."

"So what's *that* then?" Tamara pointed to the notebook, seeing her mother's handwriting on the open page.

"My notes. What I've learned so far. I wanted to be ready before the school year started, to arm you before the other kids reacted. Sorry it took me over a month. And sorry about Brenna."

"No big. She was always a bitch anyway."

"Tam—" Her mother scolded her with words, but Tamara knew there was no sincerity in it, only habit.

"What? You know it's true. I'm more upset about Madison, and *maybe* Amber."

"Well, we'll learn what we can and maybe you can

talk to them. Fix the damage Brenna did." She glanced down at the notebook. "Anyway, I only knew what they taught *me* in school—almost twenty years ago—and what's on the news. Neither of which is truly *unbiased*." She rolled her eyes and shook her head ever so slightly at what she'd often voiced as *nonsense news*. "Try not to believe everything you hear, okay? Double-check in a couple different places to be sure."

Tamara nodded and leaned forward. Her curiosity overpowered her desire to be snarky and her expression changed to solemn attention.

"For instance, we *aren't* a living myth, because we were never *actually* a myth. We were real. *Always*. As far back as documented humans, *maybe* further according to some sources. But we were turned *into* a legend and then myth by the superstitious, before we had science to explain things. Kind of how they used to bury people alive because they didn't understand comas. The first scared humans cast the lamians out of their homes and lands, and forbid them from returning under the threat of death. The lamians society continued, just in secrecy."

"Why don't they teach all that?"

"Because history is dictated by those who write the books." Jacqueline smiled.

"Well what else don't I know? I mean, I know I don't *have* to drink blood. I…" Tamara paused and blinked several times at her mom, "I don't, *right*? We don't *have* to drink blood, do we? Isn't that what the pills were for?"

"Yes and no, either those or diet. The pills were an amino acid replacement, which is easier than controlling the levels with diet for those who don't pay attention to what they're eating. We don't all eat healthy as *humans*, why would lamians be any different. But the pills are like how some people with diabetes *can* control it with their food choices, but others need a shot or a pill."

Tamara nodded again, following along and finding she was actually interested. "Oh, okay. So I'll get pills? No. You said, no."

"I *said,* we would talk to the doctor and go from there. It may be easier, but I've always hated being dependent on a pill, and if we can balance our needs with diet, I'd rather go that route. Or at least learn how, in case we're ever without the pills."

"What else did you find? I mean, that they don't tell us?"

"Actually, I found a… well… it's not a *support* group. Not really. But you could call it that. It's part of the Lamian Council who helped create the Stoker Treaty. You know all about the Treaty, right?"

"Yeah, yeah." Tamara waved her hands to indicate no big deal. "An internationally recognized set of civil laws sanctioned by the UN and all its members. Guess what's on the Social Studies syllabus, Mom? Every. Year." She rattled off the definition in monotone, no longer hearing the recited words that had been pounded into her head.

"Don't knock it kid. You need to know your rights, so you know when they're being violated." She looked at her daughter disapprovingly and Tamara could almost hear the unspoken *tsk.*

"I suppose. Fang-haters and all." She acquiesced with a nod and rolled her eyes. "So this support group that's not a support group?"

"They were hidden, but they've always known what they are and have documented their full history. They've opened their doors to a weekly meeting of sorts. Somewhere those with loose teeth, or new teeth, or even just DNA results, can go and ask questions and get comfortable with the truths rather than the hearsay. So it's *like* a support group."

"When does that start? Can we go?"

"Oh I think it's imperative we go. But it's not new. Evidently, they've been holding these meetings for almost twenty years—since the Treaty."

"Cool. So there's like really *old* vampires there?"

"Lamians. Don't call them vampires, hon. You *know* better. That's ignorant and derogatory. You'd never call your friend Brenna a nig—"

"She's *not* my friend anymore. But no. I wouldn't. Not even now. Not her or any other black person. It's a gross word."

"So is vampire."

Tamara nodded and put her hands up, palms out to her mother in a surrendering apology.

"What actually happened with you and Brenna?" Jacqueline narrowed her eyes, and Tamara knew her mother was questioning a friendship started in kindergarten.

"These." Tamara curled a lip and tapped her new eyetooth. She ran her finger down the length and felt the tip. "They're not even sharp, are they?"

"They don't seem to be, but maybe that changes with age, or has diminished with time, like our pinkies getting shorter. I've noticed some famous lamians have longer teeth, and some look *really* sharp."

"Wait, what? Our pinkies are getting shorter?"

Jacqueline laughed, "Yeah. They are. Ask Mr. Bloomfelt, I'm sure he'll explain it and waste an hour of Biology for you."

"Speaking of, I'm going to be late. Can I take this and look through it?" Tamara stood and reached for the notebook.

"Absolutely. But bring it back in one piece, okay?"

"Of course, why wouldn't I? Meet you in the car."

Tamara shoved the notebook into her backpack roughly, dropped her cereal bowl into the sink without rinsing the remaining milk, and slammed the back door on her way out.

Jacqueline shook her head and muttered to an empty kitchen, as she stood and grabbed the keys. "Because you're an excitable teenager on a mission..."

TWO

Andrea didn't hear the door close behind Dillon as he headed off to school. She was immersed in her morning routine of absorbing *everything* the couch crew on *Fox & Friends* whispered in her ear. From the breaking news of early morning perils, to the recaps of overnight events, she listened to it all as if it was the gospel and she was the congregation. On some level, she really thought they were her friends.

At least they tell me the truth.

She was so intensely fixated on the final news segment, as if it personally affected her, she spoke out loud, shocked by the *audacity* of protestors picketing a bakery. As the blonde news anchor said, "Simply because the shop owners were practicing their *God-given freedom* and refused to make the wedding cake for a lamian couple."

"But they have their *own* businesses!" Andrea shouted at the television as if they could hear her or her justification for anger. "Their *own* bakeries. Ain't no reason for them to be ruining the reputations of the hard working human businesses. Why don't they use their own stores? Stick with their *own* kind. Go *back* into hiding. Maybe then America would be great again."

The program was wrapping up and one of the men mentioned catching the special the night before about the doctor all of the women in her church group were calling Dr. DNA. She perked up, her interest immediate. She reached for the remote, grabbing at it with the jerking motion of someone taking their anger out on inanimate objects. She searched for the show in her *On Demand* menu and changed the station, as the school bus drove past her living room picture window.

"Dillon?" She raised her eyebrows as she looked around the empty house. She hadn't even thought of him as she'd been loudly lamenting the downfall of society based on the freedom of choice and power of God given to pastry chefs.

"Their own kind…" She muttered at the television, but the words were meant for the teenage boy whose face filled various frames along the walls. She glanced up at his latest school picture and let her eyes wander across the photos leading toward the stairs, the years spanning the faded paint.

The photos were a mixture of studio—or rather traveling photographer pausing at one of the local department stores—and snapshots blown up at photo centers and displayed in cheap frames. There was a great picture of the two of them at the beach, the water as blue as their matching eyes. Another of them with Dillon's first pet, a cat they called Chaos, who ran away less than a year later. Andrea almost smiled at the boy and his cat, remembering how little Dillon would compare his jet-black hair to the cat and ask if it was his brother.

He was an adorable little boy.
But now… Now he's…

She let her thought trail and moved to the next set of pictures, Christmas with matching sweaters, Halloween in costume, and a random photo she'd liked at the time for the pure smile on Dillon's face as he stood next to the car and looked back at her. That car.

Her beloved Saturn had come out the year Dillon was born, but was no longer being made. It was as out-of-date as Dillon claimed Andrea's beliefs were, and parts were as hard to find as her compassion when it came to all things lamian. It was a good car, powder blue—as strange and striking as her eyes, but much paler, softer than the anger now living in her baby blues. The Saturn had never failed her.

Unlike Dillon.

A decade and a half of images—moments and memories from their lives. Dillon. His mother. But *no* signs of his father. None. Andrea had kicked the man out when Dillon was only a toddler, *after* he'd revealed he was lamian, and she refused to speak his name ever again.

Her immediate anger and confusion at his normal looking teeth turned into a growing obsession. An unhealthy preoccupation with everything *vampire,* rather than lamian. Everything wrong and presumed, including the rumors and point-blank fiction. She mixed the truth with all the rest and considered it *all* her gospel. The lamian were evil. They were *not* of God. And she wanted nothing to do with them.

She'd spent the next decade praying nightly, hoping her sweet boy would grow up and remain human. She begged the crucifixion at the front of the church, as well as the statue of Mary near the back. She had recited so many Hail Marys and Our Fathers, even doing her Rosary during TV commercial breaks when she watched television—if pious desperation were rewarded, she should have been.

But the boy's eyeteeth had come loose and fallen free late last spring. His new teeth had finished growing in. Their sharp little white points visible when he smiled now, and her panic grew with them.

She'd invested years into their relationship, their future, as if he would be human. To find out he wasn't was a slap in the face she was still reeling from. And which caused her to openly debate whether he was a monster.

Or waiting to become one.

She'd caught herself telling Dillon the little things she did for him—pointing out the care she'd provided over his lifetime, the thousands of meals she'd made, the sacrifices she'd endured—as if she could rattle off the reasons he shouldn't kill her and drink her blood. He'd only stared at her in confusion the first time. The second time he'd laughed and pulled her into a hug, his mouth so close to her throat she thought she'd die of fright before he ever bit her. But he didn't bite her. He *claimed* he didn't *want* to bite anyone.

"What you're suggesting Doctor, is genocide. Pure and simple."

Andrea blinked and looked back to the television. The show had started and she'd missed the beginning while wallowing in the lies and empty future of the memories displayed on her walls.

"Not at all. It's simply allowing God's disciples to choose *His* creation." The doctor smiled, his teeth almost luminescent from professional bleaching.

The reporter and doctor sat across a highly polished desk from each other. Their backdrop was an electronic mural of various stills from the doctor's research. The interview was meant to look relaxed and casual, medically sound and professional, but Andrea could hear the forced civility and feigned neutrality in the reporter's voice.

"But aren't you against abortion?" She leaned forward and cocked her head at the doctor.

Andrea immediately dismissed her as a *whack-job liberal*, based on nothing more than the shocking streak of bright pink running through her hair at the temple.

They'll let anyone pretend to be a reporter these days.

"I'm against aborting *humans*. But that's why I'm

developing this embryonic test for the recessive gene. If we know whether it's human, we can make an informed decision."

"But a person can have the gene and never trigger. They can appear, for all intents and purposes, as a human for their entire life. Isn't it true the distinction between human and lamian is really nothing more than a genetic deficiency morphed into a myth of murder, mayhem and madness? Having a genetic difference doesn't make you *inhuman*. It isn't something you should strike from nature. I don't see you offering to do this for people with the Alzheimer gene, or autism or Parkinson's."

"People with Parkinson's can live normal lives for decades. And those people are still human." He looked at her as if she was stupid, and Andrea nodded, agreeing with his presumed assessment.

"You say this as if lamians are worth less, *devalued* as citizens because of an enzyme deficiency. That's like saying kids who are allergic to peanuts aren't people."

"No, no. Not at all. I make no assumptions either way. I am simply trying to provide a test for parents to achieve peace of mind. What they do with the results is not my decision." A Cheshire cat grin slipped past his practiced façade for a moment before he pulled it back into a stoic expression of sincerity.

"That's convenient. Trying to remove yourself from the use and only provide the tool?" The reporter seethed openly at the man with her rhetorical question, and then she looked at her notes and smirked. "And when will this test be available?"

"We're hoping the trials will be completed by the end of December and we'll have approval for the publicly available product by January."

"Is that because your wife is pregnant with donor

sperm and she will reach the third trimester in late December, and thus, under the current laws, *unable* to abort if you find out she's carrying a child who holds the recessive lamian gene?"

The reporter smiled, as the doctor froze—as he was obviously unprepared to address her knowledge of his wife's condition.

"I…" He blinked as his mouth hung open.

"Is it not *also* true that you belong to a group of influential people who are currently gathering their resources and contacting various lobbyists in hopes of getting legislation passed to—"

"Now listen here, little missy. There's a science to this issue. It's not only a social cause, or a matter of people feeling good about themselves. These creatures are genetically different. They lack vital enzymes, which requires them to drink blood, to eat raw meat, and to live longer. The criminal element among them sees this as a reason, a way, a *logical excuse* for violence. There's no point to purposely giving birth to a criminal." His voice raised in both fervor and pitch as he spoke, a spray of spittle punctuating his words.

"Creatures? These *creatures*? Really? You do realize they are legal citizens with rights. The same rights as you and I. They are *not* creatures, they are so closely related to humans you cannot even tell them apart unless you ask…" The reporter narrowed her eyes. "Or give them a genetic test."

"A well-trained monkey, shaved down and put in a suit, isn't automatically entitled to the same rights as a human." The doctor clamped his mouth shut and sat back suddenly—the ramifications of what he'd said swam across his wide-eyed gaze as he glanced from the reporter to the camera and back.

The reporter's eye widened enough to see the whites around their green center.

"I can't…" The reporter stood, pulled the small mic from her collar, dropped her notebook on the seat, and walked off camera.

The show cut to commercial while Andrea stared at the television, her mouth agape in shock.

"That girl baited him. Pushed him. How *dare* she?" Andrea spoke as if there were someone to hear her, to agree with her. "This doctor was trying to provide a valuable tool to would-be parents. A test, that had it been available at the time…"

Andrea's comments turned to inner thoughts, as she realized, if the test had been available, she would have gladly taken it. And upon reviewing the results, she would have absolutely gone to the clinic over in Springfield. But the test hadn't existed when Dillon was conceived. And she had no way to know or react.

Or rather, she couldn't react *then*.

Perhaps it wasn't too late to react *now*.

Maybe she could take care of the problem, *before* he became a monster.

THREE

The precinct was unusually quiet after lunch, especially for a Friday. The phones were silent, foot-traffic through the building all but nonexistent, and the rank and file quietly processed their mornings while their bodies worked on digesting their food choices. Whether it came from home, around the corner, or the vending machines down the hall, lunch had come and gone. Tupperware containers were rinsed, sandwich boxes were discarded, and the crumpled bags of guilt were shoved down to hide among the refuse in trashcans. *Everyone* was back to work. The silence of diligence and concentration left the air in the station as empty as the break room.

Detective Connor Murphy flipped through the Sherman case in preparation for the upcoming court appearance. Studying the notes and photos, he had tuned out the quiet of the desks around him. A shadow crossed his desk suddenly, and he visibly jumped as it gained a voice and broke the silence of the room.

"Hey Murphy, Chief says you get this one… since you love 'em all *soooo much*." Jasper, the newly transferred officer, snickered through the overly thick mustache he openly referred to as *glorious*. Connor was sure the man was single, but doubted he was lonely.

Connor couldn't tell if the snide chuckle was because Connor had jumped or because Jasper was gleefully dumping an unwanted file on another officer. Rather than handing it to him, Jasper dropped the pristine manila folder onto Connor's desk, covering the Sherman file as if it were unimportant. Detective Murphy sighed as he immediately recognized a fresh case by its crisp edges and lack of a label on the tab. If he were *lucky*, it would at least have the scene sheet inside.

"You know, it's not that I..." Connor shook his head and rolled his eyes as he looked up at the other officer. "Never mind." He pointed to the file with an open palm. "What is it?"

"Vamp victim—what else? Bloody and torn up and *all* you."

"Wait, a murder and I get no assist on this?" Connor turned toward the glass wall of the chief's office and sat up taller, waving the file in the air. The blinds closed in response.

"Guess *that* means the usual." Jasper turned and walked back toward the front of the room, shrugging it off as Connor's problem now.

"Do it yourself or prove you need manpower." Connor murmured under his breath as he flipped the file open and looked over the scene analysis.

Erik Smith—the name of the victim—didn't ring any bells. The picture procured from his driver's license didn't look familiar. His neighborhood was literally *the* tracks that divided the social classes of Riverside. And according to the scribble at the bottom of the page, the scene had already been processed and the body was downstairs.

"Shit." Connor pushed his chair back and grabbed his suit coat. He hated dealing with scenes after the lab crew had been through them.

"See? This is *exactly* why I keep saying we need a registry."

Connor's head turned slowly toward Detective Pattee. In a town small enough to force *every* rank in the building to share and drive the marked squad cars, there was only enough money for two detectives on staff. Most days, Connor would gladly take the entire burden, if it meant transferring Pattee elsewhere.

He looked the man up and down. Pattee was the same age as Connor, but the lines in his face, matured by hate, made him appear older. He was tall and too skinny, with tight mean muscles and a haircut that screamed, "In my spare time, I drink skunky beer and write in the margins of *Mein Kampf*." Connor was convinced he was only a cop because the military wouldn't take him.

Asshole. Why does he want to make a big bad list of hate this time?

Pattee looked from Connor's eyes to the file in his hand, and Connor realized the other detective had taken his cursing as having something to do with the *perpetrator* rather than the crime scene itself. He scowled at the man, hoping to stop Pattee's well-known cyclical argument before he suggested something stupid like a Vamp Klan again.

"*What?* Just think how *easy*… I mean, if they were all on file—"

Goddamnit, here we go.

"So you're gonna start arresting people based solely on dental records? Just because they have teeth, they *must* be criminals? That's profiling, asshole."

Officer Pettijohn interjected. "Hell yeah, and maybe we can start by rounding up all the psychics."

Connor turned and looked at the young officer who'd spoken up to side with Pattee. Pettijohn was so green he hadn't figured out how to fill out most of the paperwork, let alone shave without the need to dot his face in tiny pieces of toilet paper. Connor didn't have the time or patience for either of them, but his annoyance boiled up and fell out of his mouth without care.

"You understand both humans *and* lamians run those businesses, right? And more than half the time, when someone's *pissed off* at a psychic and claiming they're a lamian using their *gifts* against them, it turns out to be *human* scum." He sneered and shook his head. "Maybe you should stop listening to those hate-filled podcasts on your lunch breaks."

Connor strode to the front of the room and froze at the captain's desk, ignoring the still dropped shades of the chief's closed office. He waited for his superior to look up at him. Captain Harris reluctantly acknowledged Connor over the top of his reading glasses and shook his head. "Don't have the extra manpower right now, Murphy. You know that."

"Not even Adams?" Connor glanced toward the officer sitting at the corner desk.

Adams looked up at the mention of his name. He had put on some weight since being assigned to desk duty, his punishment after questionably discharging his weapon during a routine traffic stop. Paperwork whenever even *one bullet* was expended was bad enough, but poor judgment on Adams' part and the car's passenger streaming the whole thing on Facebook live had almost cost him his job. He was off the streets for another ten months. Judgmental and racist, he was still a good cop. Connor could use him internally if nothing else.

Captain Harris raised both eyebrows and shook his head ever so slightly. The shock at Connor even suggesting Officer Adams was unspoken, but loud as hell.

"Did anyone even look at this file? Body left for days. No witnesses. This isn't cut and dry." He looked the captain in the eye. "And I get no one?"

Captain Harris answered with impatient silence.

Connor huffed as he spun on his heel. "I'll be

downstairs."

"Find something worthy and I'll give you Pattee," the captain called after him, the lilt in his jest unmistakable.

"Jesus… *never mind.*" Connor walked from the offices and past reception in time to dodge a shoe flying toward him from his right. "What the—"

He turned and saw a mess of a man handcuffed to the metal bench next to the processing room, both shoes now missing from his feet. Behind him, Connor heard snickering.

"Look, it's *another* case for you." Pattee walked past him, heading to the bathroom.

Connor yelled out after him. "No, *that* is a dick. You should recognize your own kind. Plus, look at this guy—I only stick up for the innocent."

Pattee waved a hand to dismiss Connor's argument and disappeared behind the door to the men's room.

"Who says I'm not innocent?" The man leaned forward, straining against the cuffs. He looked at Connor with wide eyes and then licked his bottom lip.

"Seriously, dude? You actually have dried blood all over your face." Connor moved his open hand with splayed fingers in a sweeping motion in front of his own nose.

"Yeah… it's not as clean as you would think." There was a calculated wildness to the man's eyes.

"I'm sorry. *What?*" Connor had started to walk away but stopped and turned back.

"Hollywood always shows it as two pretty little puncture wounds." He tapped his neck with his index and middle fingers like snake teeth. "And then they suck the blood and that's it. All graceful and *romantic*. But that ain't how it works. These teeth," the man curled his lips to show his bloodied mouth. "These aren't sharp like that.

You have to actually *tear* the skin on their throats to get anything at all…"

Connor felt his lunch flip in his stomach and turned away, not giving the man the satisfaction of knowing he'd affected him. Regular criminals—murderers, rapists, drug dealers—he could deal with, but the reality of true lamian-on-human murderers, any lamian murder for the purpose of blood or meat, was that they were basically cannibals.

He whistled at the desk sergeant to get his attention and pointed behind him at the bench while holding the folder up. "Cut and dry?"

"Nah, he's not yours. He was caught eating neighborhood pets."

"Eating?"

The sergeant nodded with a look of bemusement on his face.

Connor shook the idea free and turned away in time to see Pattee exit the bathroom. He pivoted toward the stairs, not wanting to wait for the elevator in his need to get away from the man in the cage and avoid the other detective. *Asshole.*

Connor had a packed afternoon ahead of him. He needed to go downstairs and talk to Rogers about the victim, then head over to the scene and likely re-catalog the whole thing. He glanced at the clock above the stairs.

Shit.

And he needed to be at the school by 3:30.

It's going to be one of those days. He turned his body at an angle and took the stairs two at a time.

— FOUR —

"I *don't* want to see it." Madison clamped her mouth shut and huffed through her nose, almost snorting in response to Brenna's suggestion they check out the newest movie version of *West Side Story*. She only half-heartedly argued the value of the movie itself, her mind elsewhere as she ran her tongue over her tooth again.

Madison had lost track of how many times she'd surveyed the canine in the last week. Her tongue was developing a sensitive spot and the tooth wasn't getting any more stable in her mouth. It freely swung back and forth when nudged, and she swore it spun all the way around in the socket the previous night. It was going to fall out at any moment, and she dreaded it happening at school, or around friends.

Then they would know.

"Come on. Seriously, Maddie?" Brenna turned her attention back from the bus driving off with Tristan inside and slouched her shoulders in an exaggerated movement, bouncing her curls. Brenna's new hairstyle was barely an inch shy of her shoulders and Madison briefly wondered if it wasn't a practiced move to animate her meticulously stretched and twisted black hair. "But you were Maria in the play last year. And now you're telling me you don't want to see the new remake?"

Last year? Madison thought. *A lot has changed since last year.*

For starters, she hated how Brenna had grown so much taller over the summer. Even though Brenna's phone case and handbag were beyond-her-budget name brands while Madison's were knock-offs, they used to at least *feel* like equals—looks, abilities, popularity—but now it felt like Brenna talked *down* to her because of a growth spurt. Brenna was suddenly taller, with shorter even more perfect hair, and more makeup—a lot of purple had shown up on her eyes and matching nails lately. Madison, in comparison, was now a *dirty* lamian.

"But Brenna, they *changed* it." It almost sounded like whining as she stood her ground vocally, physically, while mentally scrambling to keep her secret safe. "Why'd they have to change it? It was perfectly fine when it was about *gangs*."

"Yeah well, the West Side grew some fangs this time!" Brenna laughed at her own comment and held up what was referred to as *finger-fang*s—using her index and middle fingers in a folded down peace sign, or as the ending portion of an air quote. She wiggled her finger-fangs and threw her head back in an over-exaggerated extended laugh, like she did whenever Tristan was around.

That was the exact response Madison was dreading. To Brenna, lamians were a lower class. They were all *vampires*—creatures to be ridiculed at worst and romanticized in all the wrong ways at best. Though Tamara and Amber were never vocal about it like Brenna, and stretched from upper-middle to lower-middle class, they played along whenever Brenna reminded them they were still *well* above lamians.

As a lamian among them, she wouldn't last a day of their badgering. She'd be driven from the only group of people she'd ever known. They'd been friends since kindergarten, and they'd survived everything from Girl Scouts, to camp, and eventually puberty and the boys who followed. They'd been through it all, and she knew they'd dump her the second they found out about her teeth.

"What the hell is up with Tristan on the bus? Daddy take away his shiny car?" Madison tried desperately to change the subject and bring it back to Brenna.

Brenna and Tristan had been dating off and on for almost two years. They would have fights leading to a three- or four-day breakup, but they always ended up back together. Brenna usually acted like a victor in some big battle, and Tristan often looked like a victim silently pleading for help. No one helped him. He knew what he was getting into with Brenna, and most of the time they seemed made of the same mold.

"No. It's in the shop getting a tune-up. Nice subject change though." Brenna raised an eyebrow at Madison. "Come on. Seriously, why won't you go? Amber said she's on board, but it's always better with more than two of us."

"It's stupid. They don't need to remake every single popular classic and recast it with lamians. Why not make *new* movies. Give the lamians their own voice, tell their own stories, instead of shoe-horning them into characters and situations written for humans?"

"Their own stories? Are you...?" Brenna's eyes widened and her lipstick-smeared smile twisted into something of a dare. "Why, Madison Hayward... Are you becoming a vamp sympathizer? Going to start marching with them and demanding we respect them for who they are?"

"No." *Yes*, Madison thought. "I just... I think there's enough versions of *West Side Story* for the next millennium or so."

She could hear the thinness of her argument and worried her expression would give away her internal struggle. She huffed and jutted a hip, putting on a show for Brenna. "I don't like *any* remake, Bren, you know that. And remaking a movie for *that* reason? It's stupid. Hollywood is trying to cash in on a new fan base in the name of diversity and I'm not buying into it. You give them your money if you want to, I'm out."

Madison turned away from her friend and looked down the driveway loop, praying Brenna's mother would arrive and save her from this conversation. She saw a police car enter the student pickup area and glanced left in time to see Tamara wave in her direction—all bubbly and polite, even though Madison had gone along with Brenna's lead and been cruel to her oldest friend.

Tamara and Madison had met in preschool and immediately became tight friends—a full year before either of them met Brenna. But Madison hadn't talked to Tamara so far this year. Not after learning she'd lost her canines while away for summer break and sported a new set of fangs. Brenna had pushed Tamara from the circle within a week of the news spreading through town, openly discarding her with the comment, "Being a cop's kid is bad enough, but a vamp to boot?"

Brenna's nose literally lifted so high when she turned away from Tamara—dismissing her with words *and* gestures—Madison could clearly see up her nostrils. Madison peripherally caught Amber take a physical step toward Brenna. Madison glanced between her friends, two to one, and then chose.

Poorly.

Since then, if Tamara had come close enough to see it, Brenna would make an L with her thumb and index finger and put it on her forehead. The Social Studies teacher explained how the hand gesture had once meant *loser*, but had been borrowed and evolved to mean *lamian* to the younger generation. It was still mean. Still hateful.

And Brenna did it every chance she got.

It had only been a month since Tamara had been pushed from their circle, but if she'd known then what she knew now, Madison would have sided with Tamara. Now she worried what that meant, what it said, about her. Was it because she was lamian and needed an ally, or was it because she truly missed her friend and knew Brenna had been wrong? Madison was unsure how much of her wish to turn back time leaned on one answer or the other.

The police car came to a stop at the curb and Tamara pulled the front door open, smiling as she spoke. "Hey Dad, can't you pick me up in the SUV like a normal parent?"

Madison couldn't hear if Tamara's father had responded and turned away from the grinning girl in the squad car, in time to catch Brenna's glare. Madison braced herself for Brenna's hateful tirade, but she was surprised when the girl squinted, curled a lip, and nodded at the door at the far end of the entrance loop rather than the cop car.

"What a freak."

It didn't take Madison long to find the source of Brenna's disdain, as she watched the school janitor drop his eyes to the ground and retreat into the shadows inside the building.

"Can you believe him? He was just sitting there, staring at us."

"Was he?" Madison turned back to Brenna, glad to be off the hook for the silent exchange with Tamara. "Or was he looking for someone?"

"He was staring. You *know* he was staring. He's *always* staring. Watching us in the halls, looking through the glass in the doors, and now out here. He's a *creep*." Brenna abruptly walked toward and right past Madison, as she headed for her mother's rose gold SUV. "I'll call you later about what time we'll go to the movie."

Madison opened her mouth to once again refuse the offer but left the words unspoken. She wished she could ignore Brenna's call, but knew she couldn't avoid the girl all weekend without a good excuse.

I wonder if I can get Mom to make food poisoning for me...

Madison turned to head down the sidewalk leading her off school property and headed home. She didn't notice the janitor was still watching her from behind the glass of the school's vestibule.

── FIVE ──

Henry turned the shower off and quickly ran the towel over his body before wrapping it around him. He'd thought of nothing but the blood while mowing the lawn. He'd relived the collection, *the kill*, while showering. And now he needed to reward himself with a treat.

Heading straight for the kitchen, still in the damp towel, he could almost taste the excitement awaiting him in the fridge. He reached in and pulled a pint-sized Mason jar free, and then felt his stomach flip for a moment.

"Uh…" He groaned.

He hated the way it looked when it separated. The bottom layer had become a thick, dark, almost gel-like substance. The upper layer was a sickly, blood-tinted yellow, topped off with what reminded him of the gentle froth of a freshly poured soda.

Henry looked at the other small jar and saw it had also separated. The *first* jar he had collected hadn't done that. It had stayed nice and smooth for much longer. He briefly wondered why.

Was it something to do with the size? I'd used a larger jar the first time—a big pickle jar.

He had since gone shopping for canning jars, convinced he could still smell the vinegar from the dill pickles rising above the blood when he opened it. But seeing this—the coagulation, separation—made him decide to more *thoroughly* clean the pickle jar and have it handy for the next time.

Meanwhile, he pouted and wished he hadn't gone

through the smoother contents of the first one so fast. *It is what it is*, he thought. He stood and focused instead on the blood he had in his hand.

The jar was cold and the blood inside refrigerated to a chill he didn't enjoy. He preferred it warm when he was drinking it plain for a quick treat. Or at *least* room temperature.

When I'm cooking with it, it doesn't matter.

He glanced at the stack of Internet printouts on the table and smiled at the recipes. He knew he'd find something fun to make for dinner later, but for now, he returned his attention to the jar in front of him.

Taking the metal ring off and prying loose the flat top underneath, he held the jar up to his face and inhaled deeply. Coppery.

Barely, he thought.

It didn't even smell right when it was cold and separated. He put the jar in the microwave and pushed the thirty-second button.

Just enough to take the chill off, but not cook it.

He nodded his head to the beat of the glass tray, which had come off its track and was jerking and bouncing its way around the microwave. He beat on the edge of the counter with his fingertips, creating a drumbeat of excitement to go with the bumping sounds of the glass tray. He noticed the dirt under his fingernails—even fresh out of the shower—and frowned. He used them to scrape gum and dirt, *and who knows what else*, off the mirrors and desks at school, and he couldn't remember the last time his nails actually looked clean. The ding made his fingernails unimportant and brought a smile to his face, as his anticipation rose.

Henry carefully removed the jar and stuck a long iced-tea spoon into it, swirling the separated contents slightly as he stirred the bottom sludge up into the thinner liquid. *Plasma*, he corrected himself, remembering the night he'd gone online in horror to find out what had happened to his collection of blood. He poured the entire jar into the blender—a trick he'd learned that same evening.

A couple seconds on puree and it's drinkable again.

He leaned over to watch through the hole on the top. The center of the lid had been missing since it had belonged to his mother and he usually put his hand over it, but this time, he was excited. Eager. And *needed* to see it.

The machine came to life as he pressed the pulse button. A quick whirl and the coagulated blood and plasma began to blend together. Another pulse and the color smoothed out, and he could no longer see a clear distinction between the two parts. The third pulse he held a second too long, as his mouth opened with hunger and his eyes widened with fascination. The blood blended, the plasma thinning the clot back into a liquid state. It rhythmically rose up the sides of the blender and receded back to the whirling blade below as it thinned and spun at high speed. Without warning, without precedence, holding the button for too long, the blood rose too high and spurted out of the hole.

Henry jumped back as blood splashed into his eye. It completely coated his right hand when he raised it defensively. Reflexively, he moved his left hand from the pulse button to his face and covered his eye. Without thinking, he wiped at his eye with his clean palm, then his fingertips. He blinked both eyes frantically. The kitchen was washed in a red-tint and his vision blurred, as the irritant smeared across his cornea and began to sting. He turned and made his way to the bathroom to rinse his eye and check it in the mirror.

Henry wasn't expecting to be enticed by the reflection he saw there.

Sure, he'd been spattered before. None of the kills had been without *some* blood smears or at least a speckling landing on him. But this was different. This was a thick smudge, wiped across his flesh as if he'd rubbed against a bleeding victim like he was a cat looking for affection.

And something inside him *buzzed* with delight.

He blinked until tears cleared his eye naturally, no longer wishing to wash his face. Henry looked down at his right hand and back to the mirror. Slowly, in an exaggerated motion meant to mimic a mother's hand caressing him, he wiped the back of his blood-covered hand across his cheek. His mouth hung partially open. His breathing caught as the back of his fingers drew with both life and death along his jawline. His chest hitched. His stomach tightened. His groin reacted.

His mind followed suit.

Without ever looking away from his reflection, he lowered his hand and pulled the tip of the towel free, letting it fall to the floor. He stepped back and leaned against the wall.

With agonizingly slow, purposeful movements, he wiped the blood coating his palm along his erect penis, before wrapping his fingers around it. Henry explored the sensation of the natural slickness as he slid back and forth, pulling his foreskin with just enough practiced force. His breathing matching his movement, as both sped up in a halting fashion. The air felt cool against the ever-increasing heat of the pulse in his grip.

Completely enthralled by watching his own expression, his rhythm increased much sooner than it normally would in his darkened bedroom or the steam of the shower. The excitement of having both visual and physical sensations was almost too much for him to bear, and he felt the pressure building before he was ready for the experience to be finished. The telltale sensation began in his groin and moved through his tightened stomach muscles before spreading to his extremities. He looked down as he slid his other hand forward, cupping it under the tip, intent on watching as he caught his seed.

He wasn't expecting the sight waiting for him.

The friction of his movements and the effects of the open air had caused the blood to begin clotting again. Lumps of blood jelly and sticky patches of drying coagulation were suddenly slickened with self-lubrication, as he quickly ran his hand *back* down the length of his penis, spreading his semen as he went. The whitish-gray, almost translucent, proof of his excitement smeared with the blood and moistened the clumps and bits, breaking them free of his skin but doing nothing to reconstitute their liquid state. He rubbed the soft chunks along his flesh, and both his mind and body spun into a new level of ecstasy that refused to let his arousal grow flaccid. He continued to stroke himself, desperately trying to cling to the sensation and wishing he had the rest of the blender's contents in the bathroom with him.

After several minutes of both physical and mental masturbation, he conceded to the fact he would *not* be able to climax again and slowly released his grip. He sighed in resignation and slid down to the bathroom floor.

His excitement finally grew soft, and his mind was as spent as his sex. Henry closed his eyes and listened to his breathing as it returned to normal. He pulled the fallen towel over him to ward off the chill, as he mentally relived the experience. His breathing slowed further as he relaxed in the warm afterglow of the best orgasm he could remember. He leaned against the wall and drifted.

Somewhere in the back of his mind he acknowledged the fact he would no longer be simply, *only*, consuming the blood. There was *so* much he could do with it.

I'm going to need more.

SIX

"I don't know, Andrea." The woman broke her muffin in half and carefully laid it on her plate, the napkin at the edge just so, and held her smart phone over the top of the carefully arranged food. She looked up as her phone clicked the image and softly voiced her concern over her friend's excitability. The speckling of gray strands was striking against her black hair, but it made her look older than the other two girls.

"I looked it up, Paula. Have *you* read it?" Andrea leaned forward in her seat and loomed over her untouched oversized oatmeal cookie—muffins always felt like tiny cakes with no frosting and she didn't understand the point. Her incredulous stare was meant to *will* them into seeing it her way. "You realize the things in that document are to protect humans, just as much as to give *them* rights? They're dangerous. They needed to be controlled and their population tracked. What other reason would they have done that? And the *news*…"

Lynn wiped the cream cheese of her bagel from the corner of her mouth and shook her head. "I've got to side with Paula on this. My neighbor is a vam—I mean, *lamian*—and he's really *really* nice. He's lived in the neighborhood since *before* we even landed on the moon. He keeps his house and yard neat, and always helps out neighbors if they need—" Her youthful skin and ponytail worn high to mimic teen styles, paired with her innocent expressions and soft voice, made it hard to believe she was the mother of three grown boys. Her figure was much more luck and genetics, than it was exercise—or choosing bagels over muffins—and Andrea resented her for it.

"That's just what you see. What they *want* you to see." Andrea sat back and sighed.

The three of them had been going to Ruby's since they had been teens in school together, back when it had belonged to the namesake's father and been known as Ollie's. While they had been friends for almost thirty years, the only thing they had wholeheartedly agreed on in the last several had been at Ruby's—the name change was unnecessary and the new décor was hideous, but the booths were vastly more comfortable than the previous benches.

Every Sunday after church, the three of them had a coffee, bakery item of choice, and small talk. Though this week, Andrea purposely steered the conversation to more serious matters. Pressing matters.

"You know what Father Clark says…" Paula tilted her head slightly as if repeating herself to a child who should know better. "They're made in God's image. They are the children of God, just a different flock, and we should be tolerant and loving."

"Then why aren't they mentioned in the Bible? Why aren't they in *any* historical texts?"

"But, they *are* mentioned in every culture. Literally every single historic culture on the planet wrote about them under different names. We just know *now* how those accounts were twisted and wrong, villainizing them and turning them into some sort of mythical monster."

"But why not the Bible? Why not the only historical text that counts?" Andrea could feel her patience wearing thin as her composure began to unravel.

"Oh, I know this one." Lynn sat taller. "There was a show on the History Channel a couple weeks ago talking about the Bible and how there were a lot more texts written that could have been part of it, but there were too many. So apparently the church picked what to include and saved the rest in the basement of the Vatican. They've been seen and studied by scholars and other influential people in the church throughout the years, and yes, even some lamian since they became public."

"So you're willing to believe that not only did the church decide *which* words of God we should know about, but you're suggesting the vampires were in the books they didn't include?"

"Lamians." Lynn nodded. "We're supposed to call them lamians."

"But—" Andrea's frustration rose in her chest and began to flush her face. This was not the confirmation she needed. This was not the support she had expected to have. "Don't you two watch the news? They *kill* people. They kill people and *eat* them."

"Andie…" Paula only called her the nickname when Andrea was truly upset or desperately needed a giggle.

Andrea knew this was the former rather than the latter.

"Don't. Don't coddle me. This is *serious*. We're being convinced of their innocence, blinded to the truth, by those in power for *nefarious* reasons. The devil is alive and well, and walking around with civil rights."

"Why are you being so judgmental about this? Prejudice is an ugly thing, Andrea." Lynn reached over and put a hand on Andrea's.

"I'm not prejudice. Just… Just concerned…" Her voice trailed off as she watched her friends glance at each other before turning back to her with mirrored expressions of sympathy. A part of her was confused. Her feelings toward vampires weren't new, weren't unknown to them.

Perhaps I never expressed them so clearly before?

"You know who you sound like?" Paula widened her eyes as if to suggest the unspoken.

Andrea blinked at her friend, holding back a glare of resentment, and knew exactly what Paula was talking about. She was insinuating Andrea sounded like Paula's ex-husband.

He had become fixated with the evils of the *nonhumans*—he refused to call them lamians, and no one could complain as long as he didn't say *vampire*. He started harassing them in public, everywhere he went. And then he went online, seeking them out whether he knew them or not. He moved from the Internet to the real world, and he started following them. Threatening them. And while he never *did* anything, he went far enough over the line to freak out Paula. She filed for a divorce and a restraining order the same day. Last Andrea had heard, he'd moved to Springfield. *Not far enough*, according to Paula.

"Jesus, Paula. No, I'm not and you know it. I just…" She couldn't tell them the truth. "I was reading the Treaty, and watching the news, and well, it's *all over* Facebook. The atrocities they've done and gotten away with? Because we're supposed to be open and accepting and supportive?" She looked from one to the other. "Aren't you afraid?"

"Not even a little." Lynn shook her head. "Like I said, my neighbor is *really* nice. He'd never hurt anyone. And he's over a hundred years old, you know? So he's seen some pretty rough times and some of the *worst* of humanity—living through all those wars and such."

"That's just one of them, though. And again, that's what he *shows* you. Did you ever have one in your house? Did any of your boys ever have friends who were… *lamian*?"

"I actually don't know. I never asked their friends. I

also never asked if any of them were Jewish."

"That's different, and you know it."

"No, it isn't." Lynn thinned her lips in a crooked smile of concern filled with a silent condescending tone.

Paula finished her muffin and put her napkin down. "They really aren't scary, Andie. They're just, well… I was *going* to say human, but you know what I mean."

"But they're not. They're not human. They're *dangerous*. They're *violent*. Did you *see* the news about that murder last week?"

The other two women looked sideways at each other before shaking their heads in unison toward Andrea.

"His throat was ripped out. *Ripped* out." Her face distorted into an expression of fear, more for her own safety because of her son's condition than any stranger who happened to fall victim to someone who shared it.

"Andie, you really don't have to worry like this. Yes, there are some who are violent. But there are also violent humans. They've been in our news and on our streets our whole life, and you never panicked like *this*."

"Sweetie," Lynn squeezed her friend's hand, still in her own. "Did something happen?"

Andrea glanced between them. She could feel the fear brimming behind her eyes, threatening to make her cry. She couldn't tell them. They couldn't know. They would shame her into isolation.

But they had to come to her way of thinking.

She would need her friends by her side. Would need their comfort.

She blinked and lowered her gaze.

"I was attacked…" She whispered, as she began spinning a lie to pave the way to the approval she so desperately needed.

SEVEN

"So how was school?" Jacqueline put her purse on the floor next to her folding aluminum chair and settled into a crossed-ankle position.

"School is school. I'm more about this right now." Tamara dismissed her mother with a frantic wave of her hand and looked around the room, enthralled by the people.

The meeting, hosted by the Lamplight Foundation, was an informational outreach group for *newly toothed lamians*, and the small gathering was about as eclectic as Tamara could have imagined. There were people of all color, all races, some whispering in languages she recognized but didn't understand—two Spanish speaking and at least one Arabic. Their attire seemed to range from casual, if not cheap, to business suits and high-end jewelry. Even their level of comfort spread across an invisible scale from nonchalant to obviously nervous.

Tamara smiled. *It's like the doctor's office—everyone goes.*

"What?" She turned to her mother, believing she'd spoken.

"I didn't say anything." Jacqueline spoke over the edge of her Styrofoam cup before sipping the steaming coffee procured from the back of the room.

"Are you nervous? You seem nervous." Tamara half-smirked at the idea of her mother being unsettled by anything.

"No, honey." Jacqueline didn't meet her eyes and Tamara felt a funny tickle behind her ears.

Mom's nervous.

A tall black man in a well-fitted suit, followed closely by a young woman in a simple blue dress, walked up the aisle toward the front of the room. Tamara saw him touch several shoulders on his way, the recipients of his affection smiled up at him in response. The pair got to the front of the room and turned back at the audience. Rather than standing, they both sat in aluminum chairs like the rest of the crowd. The girl was obviously more comfortable. The man appeared stiff, as if he would have preferred to stand.

"Welcome everyone." The man spoke and his voice flowed like music, smooth and perfectly toned to calm anyone who may be anxious. It reminded Tamara of the old storyteller at the library when she was young. His voice had always been able to make her stop fidgeting and pay attention. This one was even more effective, as it soothed as well as calmed. Tamara felt the apprehension in the room dissipate.

The young woman was more welcoming than soothing, and smiled widely as she moved her eyes across the gathering of faces. She took the time to pause on each and every person in attendance. She held Tamara's eyes for just a moment longer than the rest and subtly nodded to her.

Does she know I'm new at this?

"We have several new faces tonight." The man spoke with a tone of authority and knowledge. "Though I can tell by your ages, only one of you is new to your reality." He too paused, his roaming gaze focused on Tamara.

Oh my God, he's talking about me. Inside, she feared everyone turning and looking at her, but his calm demeanor buried the worry, and instead she met his eyes and smiled.

"Because of the diversity tonight, I'll do a brief overview and then we'll open up to questions." He smiled knowingly. "You have very *different* levels of information in attendance."

Yeah, like nothing. I know nothing. Tamara nodded, as she rated her knowledge against the rest of the room.

"Yes, yes. So let's start." He winked at her and Tamara slumped slightly in her seat. *Is he reading my mind?*

"My name is Maximilian, though I'm currently being convinced to let you call me Max." He grimaced snidely at the girl next to him.

While Tamara was aware of mixed relationships and adoptions, which often left a child looking nothing like their parent, these two seemed to be something different. The girl's strikingly pale hair and creamy skin tone led Tamara to believe they were colleagues at best. *Maybe a student or secretary or something*, she guessed.

"I am the current head of the local chapter for the Lamplight Foundation, commonly and incorrectly referred to as the Lamian Library. We have been absorbed by and become part of the Worldwide Lamian Council. While they concern themselves with the laws and rights of our kind, the librarians have kept our history throughout the ages, recording events as they happen for future generations. We've been doing so in written form since our lamps consisted of nothing more than a burning clump of moss soaked in animal fat, thus the name of our foundation. And *this* is Victoria, my *apprentice*."

It's like he's talking directly to me. Tamara furrowed her brows and swallowed over the lump of discomfort forming in her throat.

"The Council, as an organized collective who could share, pass, and otherwise connect these records, started many centuries ago. Long before my time. Long before my grandfather's grandfather. Before Bram Stoker, or the witch-hunts, before Vlad the Impaler, and before the Crusades. As man traveled and explored, so too did the lamian, and they shared their knowledge *and history*. As far as *what* we are and *where* we came from, it has been passed down to me that the tale of Lilith isn't all that far from the truth, minus the preposterous of course."

He paused and smiled with his eyes rather than his mouth.

Victoria interjected. "I see there are questions there. We have literature, which goes into all of this with more details, available at the back of the room and on our website."

Max continued as if she hadn't broken his train of thought. "Our own scientists believe modern humans and lamians quite possibly evolved at the same time. *Almost* the same creature. But one little gene makes all the difference between Homo sapiens and Homo hematophians, and would separate us for thousands of years. Our kind was regarded as everything from demons to witches to aliens before it was finally settled on to call us the V-word, in its many forms, spellings and meanings. And please don't use it. It's been worn out in literature and abused by Hollywood. It's a derogatory xenonym to those of us who understand the truth. To those of us who *are* the truth."

"We are lamian, as they are human. Both are people—living, breathing mortals with intelligence and a shared style of understanding and communication." Victoria spoke like a schoolteacher in what appeared to be an almost rehearsed commentary, and Tamara wondered how many times they'd given the speech.

The young woman continued. "You've heard the term *lamian*, but to explain it, you simply need to understand that much like the Latin *humanus* twisted through history to become *human*—slang for Homo sapiens—lamia is the scientifically and socially morphed acceptable slang for our kind, Latin *lamia*, or the Homo hematophians."

Victoria smiled and adjusted her hands folded in her lap. "So, we're obviously real. We've been around a *long* time. And yes, your teeth are a thing. Scientists believe now pure lamians, far back in the history books, were born with these teeth—perhaps longer and sharper—and only those of mixed blood initially appeared human. The gene itself went into hiding so to say, and became rare. But if triggered, then the teeth would follow. The teeth made tearing meat and getting to those necessary proteins and amino acids much easier than the flatter teeth used for grains, which our bodies no longer needed. So yes, we're real. The teeth are real. The need for something that happens to be found in rare meat and blood is indeed real. But fiction and fable got one thing horribly wrong—you didn't die."

"No, you didn't. None of you, none of *us*, ever returned from the dead. And you are not part of any *undead* society, culture, or otherwise. Sure the tales of those coming back from the dead have some merit, and likely began an unreasonable fear that was blended into our true existence, but not because we are or were lamian. Ancient man didn't have the grasp on science we do now. As recently in the history books as the American Revolution, we buried those *presumed* dead because we didn't understand comas, and hadn't discovered and studied the Lazarus syndrome yet. That doesn't mean they came *back* from the dead—it means they were never truly dead to begin with."

Jacqueline nudged Tamara with her elbow and nodded a silent, *See, I told you so.*

As he spoke, he intertwined his fingers, the boniness

of them made it difficult for Tamara to *not* believe everything Hollywood had taught her of her own kind. But he was just old, possibly *very* old. And she reminded herself, age, not fantasy, turns the skin paper-thin and leeches the pigment. Eventually. Tamara thought of some of the older actors and actresses of color and how well they aged. Looking at Max's skin, she decided he must be well over one hundred to have actually started showing his age.

He glanced down and considered his hands as he continued. "The belief we returned from the dead is a thinly stretched result of us being kicked out of villages and towns, *dead to our families*, and considered dead by our neighbors. Had we attempted to return—if even in the cover of night to spy on our loved ones and make sure they were okay—we were *returning from the dead,* and headhunters were soon posted to be rid of us. Their duties took on a myth of their own—with any number of cultures claiming they used stakes or running water or iron nails. Eventually, anyone carrying the recessive gene either ran away or had been pushed away from society, and all that was left were supposedly pureblood humans. Until now."

"We still die though, right?"

A voice behind Tamara interrupted and she turned to see who spoke. A woman in her early twenties who Tamara thought should probably know more than her, seemed even more lost and confused by the expression of helplessness painted across her worried face.

Maximilian's mouth burst forth a short dry version of a laugh. "Absolutely. And you will, my dear. Just like all living things, we are rotting inside from the moment we're born. You can be killed in a car accident or by drowning or any type of organ failure, just as humans. But we can, and often *do,* live longer than humans—if only because of our diet. Our bodies no longer break down and absorb fruits, vegetables, or grains after the gene is awakened, and so we take most of our nutrients from the blood-rich undercooked proteins of our meats. I still *eat* cauliflower, because I like it—especially with cheese—but my body doesn't use it the same way. It's like junk food to a lamian. Water and a meat-heavy diet is all we truly *need,* the rest is merely flavor, memories, and variety. We have a need for fewer nutrients, but of those we need *more* isoleucine than humans, it's an amino acid in meat—" He stopped and studied Tamara's face for a moment. "How are you in science class, dear? Are you following this?"

Tamara was aware he was not only addressing her directly, but others were looking at her as well. She swallowed and nodded. "I am. I understand. It's a lot, but I'm following… I think." The lilt in her voice was like an excited child being told an unbelievable tale.

"Good. To continue, we can live up to two times the average lifespan of a human. Sometimes three. *Generally* though, anywhere from 180 to 200 years is considered a normal and well-lived life. I'm over 170 and feel great."

Tamara raised her hand excitedly then pulled it back down—embarrassed she behaved as if she were in a classroom. Max pointed casually at her with the flair of a dancer's open hand. "No, no. Ask your question."

"Two hundred? That's it? I thought it was *forever.*" She used air quotes on the final word.

He smiled with closed lips in an elderly, knowing but not condescending fashion. "Remember, the legends and myths and false rumors about us all started during a time when humans considered *thirty* to be old age. To them, two hundred years *was* forever."

Tamara squinted and chewed on the inside of her lip

as she contemplated the things she was being told. Her eyes flit as if going down an invisible checklist of truths she wanted to fact-check.

"And the sun? Will I become allergic or sensitive? Will it destroy me?"

"No. That and the other wonderful doctrines of myth and fiction are false. All of them. No need to worry about the sun—you can even tan if you so choose. But you cannot change shape or physical characteristic, you cannot fly, you cannot hypnotize people, and you will *always* have a reflection."

"Wait. We can't hypnotize? I thought we could convince people to *do* things." A man in the front row sounded upset at the notion he'd been wrong about this.

Max sighed and considered his words. "You cannot *hypnotize* people per se——though they may be frozen in fear for a moment if they know what you are. Convincing others of anything is more of a charismatic quality than a lamian blood trait." He glanced at Victoria with a knowing look

"So, I'm just... different?" Tamara jumped back into the conversation.

"In a simplistic sense, yes. As much as someone with a bee allergy. They look exactly like us on the outside, but need medication if their allergy is triggered. Although, a bee sting doesn't make someone start eating flesh. Our *allergy* leads us to rare and raw meats rich with blood, and humans are made of meat and blood, so they therefore *fear* we will take it from them. That we will kill them only to eat them. As if we were starving peasants and they had a full garden of fruit for us to steal." He shook his head and Tamara could see he was annoyed with the incorrect assumption—the illogical behavior based on beliefs he'd likely run across in his lifetime.

Kelli Owen

"And what do you eat?" Victoria smiled, obviously aware of the answer. "Other than cheesy cauliflower, that is."

"I actually really like lamb, and of course beef. I'm not a big fan of pork though. Never have been. Tastes funny to me when it's rare enough to be beneficial. Fish and chicken are too slimy for my tastes. I stick to the redder meats, cow and sheep and game."

"So I guess seafood…"

Maximilian shook his head frantically, squeezed his eyes shut for a moment, and made a soft *oof* noise through his nose like a small child denying the very existence of liver and onions. He held a hand up with his palm flat to her as if to block her from his view and looked out at the rest of the group. "Other questions?"

"What about the powers? I was reading the Treaty…" The woman two rows in front of her let her question trail into empty space.

"Yes, the Treaty. You should all read it. We have it printed in the pamphlet on the back table, along with a card with our address and information on it, should you want to visit or have questions and can't wait for the Monday meetings." Max lifted his arm and indicated the location with a quick flick of a casual finger. "As far as the powers… Victoria?"

"Thanks, Max. Let's see if I remember it all this time." Victoria scanned the crowd and nodded at someone to Tamara's left and then at Tamara. "As a couple of you are learning tonight, there's a tendency to be psychic among our kind. And yes, Tod, we were reading your thoughts. We don't do it often because we think it's rude, but it does prove a point to the new people." She smiled and Tamara looked over to locate the other newbie.

"We refer to the *powers* as the three Cs—clairaudience,

clairsentience, and clairvoyance. Most people are only familiar with the last one and sometimes refer to it as ESP. Let me explain each for you."

Maximilian coughed in a forced manner to get her attention.

"Oh wait." Victoria glanced at him. "To answer the question, yes, we have powers. Sometimes. Actually, *usually*. While humans have some form of psychic gift anywhere from seventeen to forty-three percent of the time—depending on your source material—lamians tend to have them ninety percent of the time. It's actually more unusual to *not* have some form of psychic ability."

Jacqueline's face twisted into an expression of deep thought—her eyes squinted as she looked at the floor. Tamara thought maybe she was also trying to remember if she had ever exhibited anything she could consider psychic. Tamara knew *she* certainly hadn't.

"If any of you question your abilities, we can assess individuals at the end of the session. Meanwhile, let me explain the three Cs." Jacqueline blinked and looked up, and Tamara realized the young woman was talking to her mother.

"Clairvoyance, as I said, is the most familiar to people. It is sometimes called ESP, extra-sensory perception, and often exhibits with what people may call *visions*. Essentially, it's a visual ability and may be through dreams, visions of other places and things, or even seeing something right there that others don't.

"Clairaudience is the next most common, and the one used by many paid psychics. This ability is *hearing* things. It often starts with buzzing or ringing or popping in your ears, but grows over time to be *messy* voices, like the static of an out-of-tune radio, whispering you can't quite make out, or conversations too far away to understand. Eventually, this becomes clearer and clearer, and with it comes the ability to turn it off, or simply ignore it. Because as mentioned, at later stages, with the truly gifted, it becomes the ability to hear the thoughts of others." She winked at Tamara.

"And finally we have clairsentience, the ability to *feel* things. This one is actually more common than people know, but it's strange and often subtle so most don't realize what it is. Have you ever walked into a room, house, building, and suddenly felt very uncomfortable, needing to perhaps leave? *That* is quite likely clairsentience. People who have this are usually quite empathetic and in touch with the emotions of others around them, but it goes deeper than that. They can get feelings about *places*, not just people. And to really round out the crazy, almost magical part of these abilities, they work on both the living and the dead."

Tamara's mouth opened in a small circle as she inhaled disbelief.

"But *that*, Victoria, is a different topic of conversation for a different day. Suffice to say, if you believe in the afterlife or ghosts or things of similar ilk, then yes, if you become psychic with one of these abilities, it works with them as well as the living." Max's focus washed across the group, not pausing on anyone but rather scanning as a whole. "However, keep in mind, these powers will sometimes *not* work with other lamians. I've always maintained these developed as a way to protect us from harm in the distant past. If we were warned of a threat against us from humans—whether it was seen, heard, or felt—we could better defend against, if not avoid, the danger. We didn't need to be warned of lamian intent—we were on the same side. It comes in handy if you feel threatened. And you will feel threatened. We are not universally welcome yet. No matter what *any* treaty declares."

He swallowed. His expression turned to contemplation. Tamara wondered if he was going to speak or simply consider whatever thought had stopped him. He spoke.

"In almost two hundred years, it's only the last thirty in which I have been hated for something *other* than my skin color. It's eye-opening and unfortunate, but it's real for now."

He looked over the room, his gaze flitting, searching, while the truth of his comment hung in the air. He stopped on someone in front of Tamara.

"Yes, we find it rude to use the abilities, but we use it in here because often people are afraid or ashamed to ask questions and this allows us to answer something freely, without having to point out who asked it. And I have found, if one of you has a question, others likely share it."

He scanned again and nodded to someone on the other side of the room. "It's rare, but occasionally lamian develop more than one of the abilities. Any other group questions before we take one-on-one?"

He paused for a long moment before turning to Victoria and nodding.

"Let's take a quick break then. There's bathrooms down the hall, some refreshments at the back by the handouts, and for you smokers, there's a designated area at the end of the building outside." Victoria stood with purpose and Tamara presumed she was one of the smokers. As if to answer, the young woman walked straight for the door at the back of the room and several others followed her.

Jacqueline held up her empty cup and wiggled it in the air in front of Tamara's face to get her attention. "Getting a refill, do you want anything?"

Tamara shook her head, intently watching Maximilian.

Max looked around the group once again and then stood. He brushed both hands down his slacks to smooth them, and then walked over to the window. His steps were light, graceful. He moved with a fluidity that comes of class, but also age. Considering his, Tamara wondered what he'd experienced in his time. She wondered if he'd tell her if she asked.

He stood taller suddenly and turned back to the room, squinting as he scanned the people still in it. His brow furrowed and he turned and looked out the window, moving his head side to side as if he were searching for something outside.

Tamara watched his face twist up in concentration, then concern, as he continued looking outside for whatever it was he was hearing, sensing.

EIGHT

Madison opened the school-provided laptop as the second bell rang, indicating the beginning of the period. She usually considered her third hour a waste of time—a study hall she rarely needed and hardly used—and generally traded it in for a free hour of playing on her phone. Today however, she planned to scour the Internet for information on her condition. Since they had free reign on seating choices, she had moved to the back of the room to protect her notes and screen from prying eyes.

As the laptop powered up, she made a mental note of her classmates and wondered if any of them were also lamian. Study Hall was a diverse gathering of nerds and losers, jocks and beauty queens. Madison's gaze flitted across each of their faces, judging them for everything other than their teeth. She stopped herself, the sharp pang of irony crawling into her thoughts, as she realized how judgment of *any* kind could ruin any one of the students in the room via social media.

Oh how easily we can destroy each other now. One post on Snapchat and Brenna had all but shunned Tamara. Madison recalled the wickedly quick destruction of the friendship between Brenna and her ousted friend.

And yet, Tam doesn't seem too fazed by any of it. Maybe the teeth *aren't a weakness, as long as the person isn't weak themselves.*

Most of her generation had embraced the trait and stood tall to declare allegiance when they were shown to carry the recessive gene. There were as many pride parades as there were hate rallies. There was an ever-increasing number of pro-lamian businesses and laws, meant to overshadow the memories of repression and drown out the cries of the social injustices suffered and survived by lamians since their exposure and the Treaty's signing. It was no longer a viable option to simply hide the truth. It was now listed on your medical records, employment files, and tax returns. On Madison's level, of personal concern to her, it was part of your permanent educational record, starting in high school where it usually presented and then following the student through any secondary schools they chose before heading out into the job force.

Madison swallowed gently at the oppressive thoughts swirling in her head. How many of her classmates had loose teeth? New teeth? How many were truly embracing their exciting new outlook on longevity and nutrition? And how many were hiding it as carefully and fearfully as she?

Swallowing, the act of causing suction in her mouth had pulled her lips tight to her teeth and gave her a moment of panic. The loose tooth barely hung on by a thread at this point, and the other upper canine had started to move in its socket that morning. It was going to be impossible to hide for much longer. She desperately needed two things: a reason to lose a tooth—*that* tooth— in a way Brenna's suspicion wouldn't be triggered to ostracize her, and the knowledge of what to do since she learned she wasn't human.

She had decided, while gently brushing her teeth the night before, she'd simply have some sort of accident. At first, Madison thought she could *get injured* at school, but knew it would cause administration involvement because they feared parental repercussion. Trashing the car seemed a bit over the top and a sure way to get her license privileges revoked. She finally settled on the idea of conveniently *falling* when no one was home to witness it, supposedly hitting her mouth and knocking the tooth loose. Her mother had been letting her go to the dentist by herself for the last two years, so she could lie and say she'd gone and they were going to put in a replacement— then keep her mouth shut and wait for it to grow in.

The second tooth would require more thought and a different approach to avoid suspicion.

I'm not human.

The thought haunted her. Her own voice repeated the phrase several times a day. She looked around her school at classmates she knew were lamian and wondered again how many more *were*, but were hiding it like she was. She couldn't ask anyone for help. She couldn't openly appear curious. Every avenue she'd thought of would somehow get back to Brenna and she'd be socially screwed. An outcast. Starting over at seventeen with no friends, and without the benefit of switching sch—

Maybe I can do that? Maybe I can convince Mom I should go to private school.

Nah…it will be in my records soon. I'll be marked.

She quickly tucked the thought back into the hat of unrealistic possibilities and focused on the screen in front of her. Madison would have to do this on her own. And she'd start here, with Google.

She glanced around the immediate desks to see who was nearby. Her study hall had been a last-minute substitution for an overbooked photography class, so she hadn't planned it with any friends. But she needed to know *frienemies* weren't close enough to spy and report to Brenna.

As a senior in Riverside High School, she at least knew of *most* of the students in her class and the juniors directly below her. The sophomores and freshmen were less of a concern, and even less of a threat. Sitting around her was a sea of faces she didn't recognize, making most of them underclassmen. The only exceptions were a football player who was too dumb to be bothered with, and Dillon Hubbard. She'd gone to school with him for as long as she could remember, but they'd never talked or become friends. Brenna had been mean to him in kindergarten, and Madison vaguely recalled Amber having a crush on him back in seventh grade—otherwise, he didn't register on her list of worries.

She turned back to the computer and typed her first search into the open space at the top of Google: VAMPIRE CURE.

The website options on the list, or at least the first three pages worth of the 1.3 million results, were no help. They all either said there was no such thing, or referenced some video game she'd never heard of, making her wonder if it was on the list of discontinued items due to the anti-lamian-hate laws.

Trying a different tactic she typed TURNING BACK INTO A HUMAN, took a deep breath and hit enter. A nanosecond later, the search engine returned enough results all saying the same basic thing. It was enough to make her feel like an idiot for even questioning it, and she didn't click any of them.

I'm not human.

The phrase ran through her head again and this time her conscious mind grabbed it and held it down. It was time to accept it and figure out what it meant.

WHAT TO DO WHEN YOU FIND OUT YOU'RE A VAMPIRE

The first result—not surprisingly and she scolded herself for knowing better—was an oversized box defining

VAMPIRE as a contemptuous term for those of lamian decent. She changed the word to LAMIAN and hit enter. The results were much better.

Apparently there was a huge library of information and help right in town. Right *here*. Screw Brenna and her circle of snitches and would-be friends. The group was part of the Lamian Council and had been around for centuries. They'd know everything she could possibly want to ask. And they provided a weekly meeting.

I can visit under the guise of a school project, so Brenna wouldn't know the truth.

And they had a website.

Perfect, Madison thought as she clicked the link to take her there.

She scanned the homepage, skimmed through the FAQ, and then went digging with the internal search engine for reports, articles and what looked like blogs written by lamians over the years. First up: appetite suppressants. Madison smiled as she realized she wouldn't have to kill people to feed. She could just eat rare and raw meat, and take pills if necessary. There was a list of local Planned Parenthood clinics and it took a moment for Madison to realize why.

Oh, of course.

The news was constantly covering the big enzyme companies and their continued fight against the FDA to prevent a nonprescription, over-the-counter version of the necessary lamian supplements. As such, a number of income-based clinics picked up the slack by offering health checks and enzyme pills to the uninsured, malnourished, or hiding the truth from their parents.

I'm not alone.

Relief washed over Madison and she felt her eyes warm and threaten to tear up. She glanced up and saw

Dillon turned backward in his chair, watching her. His arms were crossed and he rested his chin on them, quite comfortable-looking, and made Madison wonder how long he'd been watching her. And why.

He tilted his head ever so slightly in what could have been a gesture of empathy and smiled a thin, almost pained grin. She immediately looked down, blocked Dillon out, and continued digging.

Further into the website's archives, Madison found the true science behind her condition. The actual medical information they didn't seem to share or offer or teach in school. In school they taught some basic history and rough biology, but mostly it was about tolerance. The Department of Education hadn't gotten around to teaching nonhuman realities any more than it concentrated on the truthful histories of African Americans. It took a website from an organization older than the government to tell her the truth. She was *not* a monster. This was *not* a disease. Of course, that also meant it was not curable. It was a condition though, much like diabetes, and could be treated. Monitored. Controlled.

There were drugs she could take if she qualified at the clinic. But there were also lamian treats, meats and liquids she could eat while still appearing to eat the foods her mother made. And no one would know.

She jotted the name and address of the lamian group into the Notes app on her phone, *Lamplight Foundation*, and switched the search to job hunting. She was going to need to find a part-time job to pay for the things she was going to require to pull this off.

She glanced up and saw Dillon roll his eyes and turned back around in his chair, before raising his hand and asking to be excused to the bathroom.

— NINE —

Henry worked quietly as he cleaned the last stall in the second-floor bathroom of the Riverside High School. Several boys came and went—one obviously sneaking a quick drag from a cigarette in the stall next to him, only half of them bothering to wash their hands, and most of them didn't notice him. He preferred it that way. Preferred to be invisible.

Now I do, he thought.

He had hated it back when he was *in* school. When he was part of the boys flowing in and out of the bathroom and down the halls. He had hated the way they treated him, or rather, *mistreated* him in general. He'd hated how the cool kids, the jocks, the nerds, any cliché you could label—girls and boys alike—either ignored him with gleeful cruelty, or picked on him mercilessly and treated him as their own personal punching bag. There was *no* happy medium.

He only had a couple friends back then. They were a tight group and often referred to as The Losers by those outside the circle, but he didn't care. As long as they had each other they could make it through high school. They could survive their formative years.

But then he watched, as one after another sprouted new teeth. They were full of excitement and anxiety, changing, becoming something he wasn't. And leaving him behind. He watched them grow distant, choosing the perils and prejudices of the lamian label, rather than fighting to keep their friendships with him. He willed his own teeth to come loose. To let him be one of them. To let him follow his friends into a new future. To let him belong.

He'd always been awkward, but now he wasn't even on the same level as his *equally* awkward friends. He tried to pretend his teeth were loose. He wiggled them until he accidentally pulled one free—only to have his mother rush him to the dentist and fix it. She'd unknowingly returned him to the state of nothingness he'd been abandoned in. And his friends, The Losers, had joined the rest of the school in picking on him.

They singled him out.

They pushed him away.

And he'd had no recourse but to drop out halfway through his junior year.

He stopped going, as simple as that, and his mother never knew. For over a year he lied to her. He made sure to check the mail in case of truancy notices and called the school to give them a new phone number so they wouldn't call the house. The moment he turned seventeen and could do so without her signature, he signed the papers to officially drop out of school. But he continued to pretend, for her benefit. He faked going to school every single day, only to wander down to the seedier side of town and watch the lamian lowlifes, still wishing he could be one of them. He even pretended to have the stomach flu on graduation day so his mother wouldn't go and know anything was wrong.

Of course, with no GED and no diploma, he was doomed to a menial job. What better place to watch what you want to be than to work where they blossom as their gene awakens? After working fast food for a year, he applied for an entry-level position and became janitor at the very school he ran away from. Over the course of five years, he'd come to discount most humans as subpar, and thrilled as he watched new lamians come into their teeth, their knowledge, and their heritage. He imagined if they'd have stayed hidden, they were born into families who accepted it, expected it, and there was no angst at the possibility. Humans made it dirty and wrong. Humans turned nature into a social status.

Henry felt like he was part of the forgotten, hidden culture. He was so frequently the one in the background as they found out. When they either cried or rejoiced in the privacy of the school bathrooms. Alone in pain and worry, or with friends in excitement. He'd often stand and continually wipe the same sink during the break between classes when they all came and went with a rushed fervor. He was unimportant to their lives and he could watch them as a group or individually, peripherally or even straight on, without them noticing.

But today was different. Today he preferred the quiet time during class when only a couple would come to interrupt his privacy, his thoughts. He was too excited to care about them today.

Commotion in the hall alerted him a moment before the door slammed opened and two boys came tumbling into the bathroom.

"Clean yourself up, Loser, before someone sees you and I get in trouble." The bigger kid in the football jersey snarled at the shorter boy who was busy bleeding from the corner of his mouth. Neither seemed to notice Henry in the stall, even with the door open and the cleaning cart against the back wall.

"If I get in trouble, *you* get in trouble. You'll get it again. *Worse* this time. So don't bother tattling like a little bitch." The bully yanked the door open without waiting for a response and disappeared into the hallway.

The bleeding boy lurched toward the sink and inspected his split lip in the mirror.

Henry was sure he was in the reflection, but the boy only seemed to care about the damage he'd taken.

The boy sniffled but held back the tears. He spit blood into the sink and wiped the back of his hand across his mouth. He yanked a paper towel from the dispenser and wiped both his face and hand before crumpling it up and tossing it at the can. He missed and ignored it, still not noticing Henry standing there. He exhaled in frustration through his nose and left the bathroom.

Henry ran his tongue over his eyetooth and sighed as the door closed and the room was quiet again. His again.

He returned to the mirror and curled his lip up, exposing his perfectly healthy human teeth. He'd given up wiggling them years ago. He touched the bottom of the tooth. *Useless*, he thought. *They're not even sharp.*

Yet.

He huffed, as he grabbed a rag to wipe the bloodied spittle from the freshly cleaned sink, annoyed the boy had ruined his work. But he smiled when he looked down. Several perfect blood drops sat against the otherwise clean porcelain in the sink. Not spit, but drops. Pure, perfect drops of blood.

He wiped his fingertips through them and raised his hand to inspect the blood.

Tomorrow was the big day. The day he'd finally get *his* teeth. The day he'd finally be one of them.

He licked the blood from his fingers and smiled at himself in the mirror.

TEN

Dillon rubbed his fingers across the picture for what was easily the hundredth time since he'd found it Sunday afternoon. His mom—nothing if not a woman of habit—had gone to church and then to Ruby's with the girls, giving him several hours alone in the house. He took the opportunity to go through *everything*.

His mom had been acting strange lately. Stranger than normal. Almost mean, but then not. She'd scold him for something, then turn around and point out how much she loved him and all the things she did for him. Dillon couldn't figure out her problem and was worried she was losing her mind like she often claimed her mother did. Until it dawned on him.

His teeth.

He figured she might make it through the rest of his senior year, but once he was out of high school and moved out of the house, he guessed he likely wouldn't speak to him again. *Ever.* Her hatred for *any* and all fangs was not subtle or silent, and now he was sporting his own set.

A part of him was hurt on such a deep level. *His mother?* The one person who had always been in his life was now trying to withdraw from it. But she'd hated the lamians long before he'd come along, so on a strange level, he *almost* understood her shunning him—as if he'd offended her or let her down by not taking after her.

As if he could control it.

For the first time since second grade—when he'd given up asking because she had slapped him hard enough to bruise his cheek—he started to wonder about his father. Who was he? *Where* was he?

His mom had forbidden even the use of his name. No name, no images, no phone calls or visits. Over the years, everything about him faded, leaving Dillon no idea where to even begin.

Until he rummaged his way through every last drawer, box, and forgotten envelope in the house on Sunday.

At the bottom of a long, narrow box, tucked under her bed and filled with memorabilia of his childhood— grade school report cards, awards for attendance, old baby shoes, a tiny outfit that looked too small even for a newborn—he found the Polaroid. It had been stuck to the backside of the warped cardboard placard from his hospital nursery crib. Written in blue ink across the white strip at the bottom: Shawn and Dillon.

Shawn.

My dad's name is Shawn.

Shawn Hubbard, Dillon presumed, since he knew his parents had been married when he was born. Though in all his searching he never found his birth certificate and wondered where his mother hid it, in her attempt to protect him from the name typed across it.

Shawn Hubbard. Dillon rolled the name across his tongue under his breath. It wasn't an unusual name, but it also wasn't overly common. Dillon had run into other Hubbards in the area, but had never been related to any of them.

Or at least I don't think so.

And Shawn as a name feels, hmmm out of date, Dillon thought, unable to come up with anyone he knew who shared the name. *Must be a Gen-X name,* he reasoned, deciding his father should be easy enough to find among the right age group.

Dillon ignored the late-day lesson of English class and covertly searched Google on the iPhone in his lap. Held below desk level, out of sight of the teacher's rules and snooping classmates, he searched for his father on the Internet.

It had taken him two days to decide if he really *wanted* to find him. But his mom continued to get weirder, always watching hate-filled rants on television. He needed to find his father. He needed an ally. He didn't know where else to look, so he went online.

He tried the White Pages first, but he didn't find a single public listing for the name in the state. Cellphones were usually unlisted and almost no one had landlines anymore. The White Pages were as out of date as dial-up. He couldn't even begin to fathom finding him if he'd left the state, so he presumed he was still nearby and moved on to social media.

Finally remembering his old password, he logged onto Facebook, believing it would be the most logical and easiest—since the older generations still used the site. But of the three he found, none were local. And none had the crazy jet-black hair he and both his parents shared. He tried Twitter, Instagram, and on a whim, hoping maybe his father was in touch with his generation, he searched Tumblr and Snapchat. Nothing. About to give up, he did a general search for the name and *Riverside,* and he was rewarded with a couple hits.

The first was for a website called MySpace. The page was definitely his—the profile picture showed his father only a couple years older than he'd been in the picture Dillon found in his mom's room. But the site was hard to navigate and didn't look like it had been updated for several years. The photos consisted of food and books and nothing about the images or backgrounds were helpful to find where they'd been taken. He tried to dig around further, but he quickly grew frustrated with the archaic website navigation, and he returned to the Google results.

The next few were not his father—a blonde senator's official page and a girl whose parents thought it clever to name their daughter a name Dillon only knew for boys. But as he scanned the preview text of the last search results on the page, his chest tightened and he hoped it wasn't referring to his father either.

He clicked the link for the obituary and his heart sank.

What looked like a professional photo, but was more likely an ID picture for work, showed the same face as the Polaroid. The same jet-black hair. And Dillon's nose.

He'd found his father.

The punch in the gut was selfish for several heartbeats. Then it turned to confusion.

Dillon looked up at the whiteboard in front of the class but didn't comprehend what the teacher was talking about. His mind was a blanket of muddy water drowning out a storm of buzzing insects. No complete thoughts formed. Random emotions rose but quickly receded as unwarranted or unrealistic.

How can I mourn someone I don't know anything about?

A mother who didn't want him. A father who couldn't rescue him. He was no longer just the quiet, shy boy who'd always made good grades but never really made friends. He wasn't *just* a loner. He was truly *alone*. He double-tapped the top of the window to return to the search bar and changed his criteria, looking up the state's emancipation laws and procedures.

ELEVEN

Detective Connor Murphy drank the last of the cold coffee in his prized but stained FBI mug, purchased while on a tour at Quantico several years ago. He cocked his head at the file in front of him and sighed. He had read the details, several times. He had talked to the coroner, Rogers, and gone back over the house.

Something is wrong.

It wasn't the overview—an easily forgettable citizen bled dry through puncture wounds in his neck. It wasn't the aftermath—shredded by the neighborhood's stray animals and rodents. It was the lack of anger. Lack of display. Lack of purpose. As if it were done because that's what happens, like food being slaughtered for the dinner table without a second thought. Without emotion.

And it reminded him of another case with the same missing pattern—making it a pattern after all. He stood and walked to the board at the back of the open room, past the other desks, officers and detectives, and dodging the occasional chair pushed out and left in the aisle as the owner vacated the building. He looked over the board and considered the other cases hanging on the wall like paint samples a finicky homeowner couldn't decide on—some would come down almost immediately, others would stay awhile longer.

"There." He looked at the red dry-erase note, the color indicating a dead end, and looked to the name assigned to it.

"Of course." He huffed under his breath and turned,

scanning the room.

He strode to Detective Pattee's desk. "Hey, lemme look at your file on the trailer park death—the *Winter* case."

Pattee looked up at Connor, his expression one of suspicion, "Why? You planning on dumping something on me?" He flipped through the backburner pile on his desk and pulled a thin file free.

"I think it might be connected to the case I landed last week. I'll take it if it does."

"No shit? Here. Take it." He held the file out. "And change the name on that board. Good luck." The lilt attached to the wishful phrase dripped with sarcasm heavy enough to negate the sentiment.

As Connor took the file, Pattee splayed his fingers in a *hands-off* gesture, obviously glad to be rid of it. In one smooth motion, he then moved his hands in an exaggerated sweep around to the back of his head where he laced his fingers and leaned into the cradle created there. His chair creaked and Connor hoped for a moment he would lose his balance and fall straight backward.

"Thanks." Connor left the other detective and returned to his desk.

Connor had learned through years on the job and hours of research—both on his own and by attending FBI profiling lectures—serial killers tended to have a *reason*. They had a method, if not a signature, and often staged the scene when they were done, or worse, *posed* the body for police.

He flipped through the Winter file and scanned for similarities. They were both killed in their homes, with significant blood loss through the jugular region, but nothing else. Nothing. Their killer hadn't taken anything obvious, hadn't left anything for the cops, and hadn't posed the bodies—nothing. However, in both cases, the doors to the homes had been left open and the neighborhood animals had torn at the bodies before either victim had been reported missing or anything noted as suspicious. Nature had conveniently trashed the crime scene.

What's this guy hiding?

His case victim, Smith, had been unemployed, single, no living family members, no one to come forward to claim him or call him friend. The Winter file had been similar—but rather than unemployed, he had been on medical leave.

Why?

Connor flipped through the pages and found Winter had recently been part of a clinical trial group. The living room where he had been found dead was "overly gory" according to the first officer on the scene. The autopsy report noted Coumadin in the blood stream, but no other drugs—street or prescription—were found in the screening panels.

Rogers' handwriting explained further: *"this would have thinned the blood and allowed him to bleed out faster, blood spilled at the scene would have spread farther and looked like more than it was, due to the anticoagulant properties."*

There was an asterisk on the body outline page where various wounds were marked, specifically next to the indication of a wound on the victim's neck. Connor was unprepared for the significance of the seemingly scrawled and forgotten note: *NOT TEETH.*

"The wound appears to be a single puncture mark, made by an instrument at least three inches long to explain the internal perforation damage to both the thyroid and trachea. It is unlikely, if not impossible, to have achieved this damage with the much shorter suggested weapon of canines, either animal or humanoid, naturally or with dental extensions. No human or lamian saliva was found on or near the wound. The weapon in question created a uniform entrance wound in the form of a clean initial puncture. Then the flesh was stretched abruptly rather than torn as it tapered to a thickness of about an eighth of an inch. Width, length and lack of trace evidence would suggest a metallic weapon, such as an orbitoclast, or perhaps a common ice pick."

Connor froze. He squinted his eyes and his gaze danced over the words without focusing on anything in particular, as he thought through various details of the file. He flipped to the newly added coroner's report in his own file and noted it too had a stretched puncture wound of approximately an eighth of an inch.

Winter and Smith had something in common after all. Neither was killed by a lamian.

At least not one using their teeth.

He closed both files, intent on taking them downstairs to Rogers. Perhaps they'd been too far removed. Perhaps an assistant had worked on one. For whatever reason, the cases hadn't been tied together yet and Connor felt that was a huge mistake. If Rogers saw them together and agreed, maybe then Connor could get some extra manpower. Catch the killer. Close the cases.

"Hey Connor, your kid's here."

He blinked free from his thoughts and looked up to see Tamara walking through the room toward his desk with an irritated look. He glanced at the clock.

"Oooh." He stood, files in hand and gave her a one-armed hug. "Sorry, hon."

"Whatever. The station is halfway to home, so I figured I'd walk this far."

"I need to go downstairs. Can you hang here and do

your homework for a bit?"

She looked around the room, discomfort obvious on her face.

Connor followed her gaze. He saw several of the officers watching her with a sideways stare. His daughter. Accusations and judgment openly twisted the expressions aimed at her. *The lamian.*

"Um… they don't really like me anymore do they?"

He watched her flinch as if a shiver had run through her.

"I'll just go to the lounge."

He nodded, agreeing with her assessment and plan. "Thanks, hon. And again, sorry. Mom will be back on her regular schedule soon." He leaned forward, kissed her forehead, and took the lead out of the room. Looking back over his shoulder, he whispered. "If they annoy you, kick 'em."

Her light giggle made him feel better about her, but not his coworkers.

— TWELVE —

Parking at an awkward angle, too far from the curb, Henry rushed to his front door and almost broke the key off in the lock as he frantically pushed to get inside. He'd taken a vacation day and scheduled his appointment for 11:00 in the morning, believing the streets would be clear and he wouldn't waste precious time on the road. He hadn't expected the pre-lunch-hour traffic when he'd finished, and his eagerness for the next step had nearly caused him to pull over on the quiet stretch between Riverside and Springfield. Finally breaking past the people who didn't know how to pack a lunch or had scheduled their meetings over menus, he'd sped the remaining distance home.

The excitement-induced saliva ran free in his mouth and mixed with the slight taste of copper as he accidentally bit his lip. The plastic runner inside the front door, a leftover from when his mother had been alive, was sprinkled in dirt and scattered with shoes. He had no time to follow a dead woman's rules today, and didn't bother to take his shoes off at the door. He made his way to the bathroom and eagerly tore open the white paper bag he'd been given at the dentist's office.

Reaching in, while he swallowed spit, blood, and years of desire, he retrieved the box. He gasped and held it away from the sink, suddenly imagining a horrible accident. He pulled the drain stopper upward to plug the sink, to prevent a mistake his psyche couldn't afford, and laid a clean washcloth in the bottom of the porcelain to be on the safe side. He exhaled loudly with puffed cheeks and returned his attention to the box. He opened it gently and sighed.

Getting vampire teeth was not a new thing. The fad had been around long before the lamians crawled out of the pages of legends and into the streets, before the Treaty and society's attempt to accept them. People had been getting veneers when vampires still belonged to Hollywood and Bram Stoker disciples. Humans had been sharpening their natural teeth to points when New Orleans and Transylvania were romanticized destinations for parties and role-playing. They paid for wicked little dagger-sharp caps instead of braces when the underground phenomena rose in popularity based on a desire to be the fabled creature of the night. People had been making their standard, run-of-the-mill canines into the spectacular, the mythical, when it had been only a *subculture*. Now they were a genuine race, a breed of humanoid, the dentists didn't flinch. They were used to the craze, the fad, and the fanatics who came with it all—whether their desire was to mimic vampires, werewolves, or something as mundane as a tiger's bite. Now the professionals simply asked if you really *were* a lamian so they could mark your chart before they took a mold of your teeth.

Acceptable or not, commonplace or not, it was still expensive—especially if you wanted good, high-quality implants or caps. And, as an *elective* procedure, Henry's dental insurance wouldn't cover *any* of the costs. He had wanted them since he secured steady work at the school. But his expenses and paycheck didn't allow for *frivolous fangs,* as the dental receptionist had called them, raising her judgmental eyebrow in a high, overly plucked arch, as she did so. Saving would have taken him *years* on his meager salary, even with his yearly two percent raise.

But the universe *hurt* him to *help* him.

His mother's death had been unexpected, the pancreatic cancer already well into stage four when they had discovered it. The doctors could do nothing to cure it and concentrated on treating her pain, treating what they called her *end-of-life comfort*. Henry had been heartbroken, as he lost the only parent who cared about him—the only person in his life *he* cared about.

However, her brief fight and quick death had left him with more than emptiness inside him. It had left Henry with a mortgage-free home to move back into and the ability to say good-bye to the cost of rent. It had come with enough insurance money to cover the medical bills her healthcare plan didn't pay for *and* the funeral. And with the help of his paltry seven hundred dollars in savings, there had been enough left from the policy to give him the *frivolous* dental expense of his dreams.

The box in Henry's hand held his very own—cast to perfectly fit *his* teeth—vampire fangs.

Fangs, he thought. *I finally have fangs.*

He touched the tip of one, sitting in its foam cutout meant to keep it secure during travel. It was sharp. Not sharp enough to *slice*, but more than enough to puncture. He looked up to the mirror. He could see the excitement in his face. His eyes were wet with joy. His smile was genuine, broad, and—

Oh God.

Henry closed the box carefully and put it on the closed lid of the toilet. He frantically grabbed his toothbrush and paste.

I need a clean surface.

He remembered how the dentist had cleaned his mouth when he'd reset the tooth Henry had pulled the previous year—the *second time* Henry had tried to make his biology change on a whim by removing his own teeth. Henry had yanked the human tooth, desperate to force a reality that was not his own, and proudly brought it to his dentist. He had declared, "See? I'll get a new one now. A vampire tooth."

The dentist had looked at him with pity. "No, Henry. The x-ray shows nothing there. You know that. We talked about this when you lost your tooth last time. You're not a lamian, son. But it's okay. You saved this, so we can put it back for you. Again."

Having the tooth re-socketed had been more painful than pulling it out. Henry had to sit there and listen to the dentist drone on about how he could give him fake teeth, but it wouldn't change his DNA, wouldn't make him lamian. The dentist said it was a good thing. Said having a deficiency of *any* kind was more of a pain than a blessing, even if Henry thought it was a romantic notion.

The mental anguish and embarrassment of having your dentist *know* your deepest desires but stop them from happening and then chide you like a little boy, was too much for Henry. He changed dentists immediately. He was more careful about what he said and did around medical professionals after that. But he remembered the way the dentist had scrubbed his mouth and disinfected everything before replacing the very human tooth Henry had pulled out. Henry mimicked the dentist's thoroughness as he shook free from the painful memory.

Henry scrubbed his teeth until the toothpaste no longer foamed. He spit repeatedly, noticing the slight red tint in the last few blobs of spittle and watered-down foam. Finally happy with the results, or at least satisfied enough to continue, he rinsed his mouth and put the toothbrush down. Picking up the box again, he felt the warmth of tears building.

His father had been at the funeral, but he hadn't come to the house afterward. The man hadn't needed or wanted any of his ex-wife's belongings, and his new wife—his shiny new *vampire* wife—was waiting at home for him. Henry remembered when his parents divorced his sophomore year, not long after the *first* time Henry had a tooth replaced. He remembered how his mother tried to say they had simply grown apart. But his father had remarried as soon as the ink dried on the divorce papers, and Henry knew something deeper was going on.

Then he met her.

He knew instantly, but he asked with the innocence of a child, and she smiled wide and nodded. Yes, she was lamian. It hadn't dawned on Henry then how she would outlive his father by a full lifetime. He'd been too busy twisting her genetics into a self-appointed rejection by his father.

The man who had told Henry when the dentist reset his tooth, "Henry, you're just a human. It's okay."

The same man who had left his *very* human family, for a *vampire*.

Henry became enamored with his new stepmother, and he asked her many questions during his visitation weekends with his father. Too many questions, apparently, as she started having weekends away and functions to attend whenever Henry was scheduled to visit. He tried asking his father, but he caught on too late—neither of them wanted to talk about it.

"Henry stop, just stop. Be okay with what you are."

Okay? No, Henry could not just *be* okay with it. He wanted to be a vampire more than anything. They were real. Not fantasy. And he wanted to be one of them. As an already emotional teen, Henry pushed the topic with his father in all the wrong ways. Eventually, his father stopped coming to collect him. Always busy. Always promising *next weekend*.

But Henry knew. He felt the pain deep inside as it made a home there. His father had cast him aside for a vampire. He remembered the apologetic look on his father's face at the funeral, but no words were offered to back it up. The man had walked away from Henry years before, and had visited long enough to see his mother put in the ground. Henry hadn't heard a single peep from the man in the year since.

Henry looked back to the box in his hand and carefully opened it again. Slowly, deliberately, he revealed the contents as if a spotlight were about to shine on them. He couldn't remember ever being this happy and nervous at the same time. He imagined it was what people often felt in a relationship, perhaps at their wedding, or when having a baby. This was his crowning moment. The moment he would no longer be *just a human.*

He carefully removed a cap and fit it over his tooth, checked and double-checked them both to make sure he had the right one for the right tooth. He licked his natural teeth repeatedly, feeling for the last time how they felt. He looked over the instructions for application, removal, and cleaning. Satisfied he understood, acknowledging they were supposed to be *temporarily* worn—held in place with denture cream each morning—Henry crumpled up the instructions and dropped them into the small white trash can by the sink.

He grinned with delight as he reached for the *permanent* dental glue he'd found online.

THIRTEEN

Madison had told her mother she wanted to walk home, under the guise of enjoying the weather before fall kicked in and she couldn't enjoy it. Her mother, who only picked her up when she specifically asked or the weather suggested it, hadn't even questioned the request. Madison had always been athletic—cheerleading in junior high, dance class when she was younger, and currently debating whether or not to join the volleyball team this year—so her mother encouraged it, but with a strangely distant look. As if she wasn't truly listening.

When Madison turned to start her walk home—after waving off Brenna and Tristan's offer of a ride, which she declined based on *no one* wanting to be *that* third wheel—she noticed the janitor wasn't in his regular perch. Instead, Dillon stood there, watching. He watched her specifically, rather than the crowd at large as the janitor did. She found it just as creepy, if not more so, and wondered what he could possibly be up to.

She'd thought about him and his behavior lately as she walked home, which made the trek go much faster than it would have otherwise. Dillon had been there a lot lately, in her peripheral vision. Never really part of what she was doing, but there—be it in study hall, out front after school, or standing by the water fountain near her locker when she *knew* his locker was the other direction. She wasn't *bothered* by him or his presence, even if Brenna would have surely had something to say if *she* had noticed him. It was more a curiosity thing. And a strange comfort.

No, that's not it.

She tried to remember if they'd ever had classes together before this year's Study Hall and Social Studies. If there had ever been an occasion to be partners in a project or have a conversation of any sort. Outside of group play in kindergarten, she could think of nothing tied to school. Though, the image of him being upset and walking near the fountain in the park came and went from her mind, but she couldn't place when that had been and couldn't actually remember ever seeing him there. She could think of nothing else and was confused by the strange way she felt okay about him, without even really knowing him.

Madison was buried in her thoughts about Dillon when she walked in the back door of her house. Normally she would have announced herself, but between her panic about her teeth keeping her quiet in the house lately and the strange thoughts of Dillon rolling around her mind, she didn't even think about it. She dropped her backpack by the dining room table and left her jacket on the chair next to it. She took the steps two at a time toward her bedroom, heading for her old yearbooks to see what activities Dillon had been photographed in over the years.

She wasn't expecting to find her mother in her bedroom, squatted down by the bed, looking under the mattress she currently held several inches up in the air.

"What are you *doing*?" Madison's lip curled up in disbelief.

Her mother was visibly startled and dropped the mattress as she jumped to an upright position. "You got home quick."

"Mom. What are you doing?" She held her hands out in front of her, palms up, and indicated the room at large.

"I'm…" Her mother struggled to find the words. "I'm trying to figure out what drugs you're on."

"What *drugs*? Are you serious?"

"Madison, you're acting all crazy lately." Her mother took a step near her and Madison braced her footing defensively. "You don't smile or laugh anymore. You look down at the ground all the time. You're quiet."

"So I'm quiet. So what. I'm thinking." Madison felt the lie fall from her mind to her tongue. "You know, school is harder this year. I have honors classes. I have things going on."

"Are you and Tamara still fighting?"

"What? No. Tamara and I—" She huffed, she had to get her mom out of her room, her face, her business. *At least until I figure out this tooth situation.* "This has *nothing* to do with Tamara."

"Well what then? Are you taking some sort of drugs or diet pills or something? You don't eat with us. You take your plate upstairs and I find most of it in the garbage the next morning."

Her mother took another step toward her and she could almost feel the forced hug coming. Madison stepped back into the hallway.

"Mom! Jesus. Just leave me alone. I'm not doing anything. Stop overreacting."

Madison turned and ran back down the stairs and out the door. She couldn't deal with her mother on top of everything else right now.

"Madison, you get back here!"

She ignored her mother's cry for obedience.

Christ, because puberty isn't bad enough, I need a snooping mother and *a loose tooth?*

She turned and walked toward Tamara's house out of habit.

Damn it.

Madison turned at the corner and headed for the small neighborhood park instead. She'd found herself there a couple times over the years, swinging as high as possible to try and be nothing but part of the wind for a while. It always cleared her head, or at least distracted it long enough to calm her down.

The rumble of an old truck stopped her before she could cross the street and she paused, waiting for the vehicle to stop. As it got closer, she saw the occupants— some football player she recognized but whose name she couldn't remember, and the school slut, Brittany. They laughed and carried on between each other, unaware she even stood there. Unaware of the world around them in general.

Madison watched as they paused for a brief, rolling stop and then kept going, not even letting her cross before they carried on. As they drove away, it looked for a moment as if they were both covered in smears of bloody makeup, with a gaping wound on the side of the football star's head leaking brains and blood.

She shook her head. It was too early for Halloween parties, so she could only imagine they were up to no good. She watched the Ford Ranger as it drove past and squinted at the reflection of Brittany in the side mirror. In the dirty glass, it looked as if all the blood had been wiped off and she had returned to her normal, if not overly heavy, makeup.

"Whatev—" Madison's disdain immediately countered with a gasp and she raised a panicked hand up to her mouth. The single word had used just enough force between her lip and teeth to knock the loose canine free.

Using her tongue to find the nugget against her bottom gum, she rolled it out to the front of her mouth and spit the tooth into her hand. She stared at the truth in her open palm—tiny and white, with the smallest bit of blood and tissue still attached. Her tongue immediately went to the empty socket she could no longer ignore, as silent tears of panic welled up in her eyes.

I'm officially a monster.

FOURTEEN

Andrea had spent the last four days trying to justify the lie she'd spun to her two oldest friends, in hopes they would see the vampires, the *lamians*, as evil on a whole. She didn't feel bad about making up a story about a neighbor who didn't exist. She wasn't upset about trying to convince them to side with her, to blindly give her permission to take care of a situation for which they didn't have the real details. But she felt *horrible* for lying to the two people who had *always* been there and never failed her.

Especially since it did no good.

When they parted ways from Ruby's the previous Sunday after church, they'd suggested she be the better person. Instead of rallying around her anger and need for action, they'd instead tried to convince her to forgive her attacker. To be kind and Christian, and to understand they're not *all* bad.

"No more than all humans are," Lynn had said as she hugged Andrea goodbye.

With nobody on her side, and the only voice of reason coming from the sources she trusted in the media, her conflicted thoughts were starting to consume her every waking minute. She weighed the pros and cons of taking action as she flipped the channels.

She would listen to what *everyone* had to say. One last time.

Even the lies of the far-left crazies.

She knew they'd all have different takes on the topic,

differing opinions, and they'd use different statistics. But she hadn't realized how insane they would sound. How far each side leaned from the opposition, as if it were a tug of war over a mud pit and no one wanted to land face first.

Fox & Friends had a guest on the couch—a senator from down south—who argued the death penalty was *completely* appropriate if the lamians were caught in the act or proven guilty. He claimed the life expectancy should play a part in sentencing.

"If you sentence an eighty-year-old man to life, he will serve maybe ten years. The same sentence to a lamian would be one hundred. That's a long time for the taxpayer to take care of a criminal. *Life* was defined on the law books long ago, which is why they say fifteen to life, or twenty to life. Life is the *outside* mark. But their lives are so much longer. If they're guilty of something horrible enough to keep them off the streets *forever*, then why waste a jail cell on them?"

Andrea understood what he was saying. But heard in *that* context, she thought it was harsh.

The punishment should fit the crime, not the criminal.

She couldn't remember where she'd heard that, but she thought maybe it made more sense than the man on her television. She found herself agreeing with it, and acknowledged the notion was about as left as her thinking wavered.

CLICK.

CNN was sounding off about social equality and giving all lamians the benefit of the doubt, believing you should deal with the problems when they arise rather than *presuming* they will and preemptively taking action. "They've been around as long if not longer than us. If they had wanted to, they could have killed us all at any time."

Andrea dismissed her as a bubble-headed blonde spouting off an obviously practiced phrase. *Who wears pearls before noon? And those dark roots? Have some self-respect before you demand it from others.*

CLICK.

The news channel, with too many letters for Andrea to ever remember them in the correct order, had a panel of self-proclaimed experts arguing the definitions of genetics and race.

"It's not a recessive gene in everyone. It's only in those whose bloodline has been mixed at some point. Like whether or not you have Italian in you. That doesn't mean you automatically like spaghetti or mob movies."

The other two men on the panel blinked at the obviously stereotypical sweep at an entire nationality and Andrea could almost hear them mentally *tsking* the man.

"At some point, far back in our lineage, the occasional lamian and human mating happened. Perhaps not even that far back for some families. And thin as the gene's chances may have diminished over the years, it was still there. So if you have the gene, and it never triggers—your teeth remain, you die before one hundred—does that make you human or lamian? How blurred is the line that they should have *different* rights?"

"Perhaps a percentage? Don't you have to have X amount of Native American in you to receive any benefits from your tribe?"

"Are you suggesting if you *might* have the gene, and it never wakes up, that you should be treated as a lamian because you *could* become one? How do you expect to control who signs up for benefits?"

"It's not about benefits. It's about acceptance. Eighty percent of the developed world has a statistical chance for carrying the gene. That doesn't mean it will trigger.

It doesn't mean they'll change on a genetic level. But you never know who could be carrying it, and should treat everyone with the same modicum of respect."

"Eighty percent? Where'd you get that number? It seems awfully high. And before the Treaty? Before they came out of hiding. Where were they all?"

"They haven't been physically hiding for years. It's not like they lived in caves. They were right here the whole time—they just didn't tell you what they were. Do you know how many teenagers run away each year? It's exponential to the population. As there are more people, there are more runaways. And I'm only talking bout the teens. The ones going through the change, the ones who are suddenly scared and confused, and it has nothing to do with their sexual hormones but with their teeth. They run and they settle elsewhere. And when their age starts to make people wonder, they move again. They found each other and helped without going public. *Hiding* makes it sound like they were out of sight. Did the homosexuals *hide* in caves before we rudely demanded to know their preference? No. They were doctors and teachers and lawyers and no one knew otherwise."

Andrea could understand and agree with some parts of what they were saying, but found she couldn't agree with any one of them completely. She shook her head at them making things more complicated than it needed to be.

It's simple. If you grow new teeth, you're a lamian and you fall under the laws set up for and because of lamians. Period.

CLICK.

A commercial for a talk show featuring a lamian with a weakness for blood, currently serving time for attempted murder, was louder than the programs had been and forced her attention. The victim had lived. But instead of going after her attacker, she sided with him and was sitting and fighting alongside him, trying to get the public to agree he wasn't murderous, but rather had a sickness. She said it was a *condition* like alcoholism and should be treated as such.

The host of the talk show smiled at the camera and asked, "Can attempted murder be considered a disease, a condition to be treated, or a common weakness? Should he be treated and released or locked up with *common* criminals?"

"Wouldn't he be a danger to them, then?" Andrea questioned the television as she changed the channel yet again.

CLICK.

A middle-aged man was wrapping up his program by leaning forward and talking directly into the camera, as if it were a personal conversation with the viewer.

"Before they came out, before we knew, they were among us. Your lawyer, your teachers, even your doctors, could have been one and you didn't know. But they knew. They had an underground. They had their own businesses and laboratories. They were secretly making the enzyme supplement for years under false documentation and borrowed grant funds, and passing it out to known vampires. To those they'd found, those on their register they say they don't have and won't share as they continue to indoctrinate us with their lies. But what of those they didn't know of. How many crimes, murders, were committed by lamians who didn't know what was wrong with them? Who didn't have the medication to help them? How many prison escapees and suicides were simply lamians who knew what they were and were trying to hide their aging abilities? Trying to hide their secret from us."

The man offered too much speculation and no direction, even for Andrea. She needed answers, not more questions.

CLICK.

An overweight man with headphones and a thick mic in front of him spoke loudly and wiped at the sweat on his forehead. His oversized voice boomed as he spewed his conspiracy theory.

"The government's been doing it for decades. Taking them as soon as they change, as soon as they become deadly. They've been training them. Training them to look and act human, to slip into anywhere they want, anywhere in the world. Their secret vampire assassins." He looked at the mic and almost panted in excited exhaustion. "You think a stupid rivalry took Tupac out? People, pay attention! He had a message *they* didn't want you hearing."

Oh my God.

Andrea was considering the rapper's death. She remembered it vividly. It had been all over the news. She didn't listen to his music, but she shared the general malaise of the country—saddened we would shoot our own for no reason. *Assassins though?* She was looking at the big picture.

Vampire assassins? They could slip into any country, anywhere in America, and look and act just like us. Play the part and wait for the proper moment, and WHAM!

She froze with the remote out in front of her, as she thought about the repercussions of an assassin squad. The government could use them, but citizens would be forever looking over their shoulders. Even more than they do now.

They could use them for more than just taking out problems. They could use them to start a problem. Start an uprising to declare the need for force.

The television and all its horrors faded, the sounds of the angry man's solo argument slowly being blocked out as Andrea's thoughts twisted further, searching for examples such as hers.

What if Hitler's mother had known what he'd become? Or Charles Manson's? She thought about the great monsters of history. *Would they have raised them knowing the outcome? Would they have waited and watched and let it happen? Or would they have taken matters into their own hands?*

Can I take things into my own hands?

Am I strong enough to kill him?

"Mom!"

Andrea spun her head, startled by Dillon's sudden voice, and worried for a second she'd spoken out loud. She blinked at him, unsure what to say.

"Did you hear me?"

"No. No, hon. What?" She hoped her eyes weren't truly as wide as they felt, that they didn't betray her fear of her own son.

"I'm going to need lunch money tomorrow. My balance is under five."

"Oh, okay." She relaxed a bit. He hadn't been paying attention. "I'll go online and make a deposit."

"Thanks." He spun and headed for the door, casually looking back at her with a concerned face, "You really should watch something less, um… *angry.*"

— FIFTEEN —

Henry woke up with a sore mouth. The glue he'd used had irritated his skin, but not as much as pushing the caps tight enough against his teeth to cause them to slide under the edge of his gum line. Tight enough to look real. The teeth were secure, but making them so came at the cost of several nicks, scrapes and a general ache. On top of that, his new teeth were longer than his natural canines had been, and they rubbed against the tender skin inside his lower lip all night long. Once awake, he left his mouth partially open and mostly avoided the sore spots, but the damage was done. Through his morning routine, his tongue constantly flicked across the sharp points of his new teeth, and when he bit down softly, he'd poked his tongue enough to cause a raised bump.

When he had habitually returned a greeting from the school maintenance man, it had been the first time he'd spoken out loud since gluing in the caps, and he hadn't been expecting his speech to be slurred. Gary paused and looked at him, but Henry put a hand to his mouth as if he were in pain and excused it as dental work from the day before.

Whenever he found himself alone throughout the rest of the day, Henry talked to himself. Not anything of importance, and sometimes only listing the items he could see in the immediate vicinity, but enough to practice speaking with the new teeth and *not* sound like he had a fresh tongue piercing. He found certain letters and words much more difficult to say than others.

He'd been daydreaming off and on all day, flicking his tongue at his new teeth, and hadn't even cared about the overtime he now had to put in because of after-school football practice.

Teen boys can trash a bathroom faster than a white uniform on a muddy field.

Now that they were gone and it was quiet, he was cleaning up the field bathrooms on autopilot so he could go test his new teeth. A vehicle in bad need of a tune-up rumbled outside and snapped him back to attention.

He turned off the light and opened the door to check the noise. A Ford Ranger had pulled into the area at the end of the bleachers, easily visible from his location in the concession area underneath them. The window on the truck was down and he could hear their voices.

"Jesus, Brittany." Henry saw the boy flinch and the truck jolted forward as he cut the ignition. "Really, girl?"

"Yes, really." The girl shifted in her seat and Henry could see her wide smile. "I told you I was horny."

"You're *always* horny. Shit, you're *known* for being horny!"

The boy turned toward the concessions and Henry quickly pulled back into the darkened doorway of the bathroom, coming up against but not knocking over the mop bucket he'd just emptied. His hand moved behind him to steady the equipment.

"Not in here. Come on." The boy opened the truck and hopped down. He turned and put a hand up for the girl, but she ignored it and jumped directly at him, knocking him backwards as he struggled to catch her and retain his balance.

"Bathrooms?" Her eyes were wide with excitement and Henry realized they were looking for somewhere private. He held his breath and tried not to panic.

"Nah, they're always locked after practice. But we can go back behind concessions. At least there's a mat back there."

She reached down and slapped his ass. "Well giddy-up!"

He turned and came straight toward Henry, past the soda and pretzel stands. The boy turned suddenly into the concession area for hot dogs, the last stand before the bathroom, just as Henry thought he'd squeal and give away his position. Instead, he had a perfect view from the tiny gap in the barely open door. He relaxed a little, exhaled, and watched the teens.

The girl unwrapped her legs and released her hold on him as she hopped down to the ground, her weight making no noise as it hit the mat in the quiet under the bleachers. She immediately undid his pants, reached in, and wrapped her fingers around his already reacting penis. He wriggled his jeans down to his knees and let her continue to fondle him to hardness, his pants landing in a scrunched-up heap at his ankles, kept there by his shoes. "You're not going to use those fangs on me, are you?"

Henry gasped in the darkness. Was she a vampire? Human boys tended to be fascinated with the vampire girls. His dad, several actors he knew about, and even a few of the school staff—it was almost as stereotypical as a jock with a bouncing blonde on his arm. And now this couple was possibly both clichés.

Brittany giggled as she expertly unhooked her bra with a flick of her fingers. "Only if you ask me to…"

"Um…" He reached over and helped her remove her shirt and loose bra. "Take 'em out."

Out? Fake fangs. Henry's disappointment was only momentary, as his voyeuristic curiosity began to spread warmth through his body.

"You talk too much." Brittany dove in and kissed him deeply, her tongue visibly delving past his teeth with a lustful hunger.

Henry recognized the girl. She'd been in his bleachers before. And in the boy's room in the school. And in the locker rooms of both the pool and arena buildings.

Slut. He immediately tagged her as his mother would have.

If she was a vampire, Henry could have excused it as simply living life to the fullest. But as a human, a fragile being who will age and die before a vampire is even settled down? *Disgusting.*

His mother had told him, "Once you have sex there's no going back to holding hands." And he'd been very careful to never overstep boundaries with women. Of course, he'd only had the two occasions. The not necessarily *unattractive* waitress who was happy to have his attention, until she revealed her true self and he realized her loneliness had turned to desperation. Henry didn't feel she was picky at all. She only wanted out of the life she'd dug herself into, and he wasn't interested in being someone's escape plan.

The other opportunity had been squelched before it even blossomed, when his ex-best friend in high school purposely went after the girl he knew Henry had a crush on—Heather. The second the fangs had sprouted on those closest to him, Henry had been abandoned by his own friends. They had nailed the coffins of their friendship shut forever by purposely going out with anyone they knew Henry had been interested in but too shy to talk to. Last he heard, Heather had two babies from two different boys, and she was with neither. *Slut.*

Sex got you nothing but disappointment.

Lust didn't need to be sexual to be sated. It could

simply be possession, a taste of someone else's life. *Or death.* Henry smirked and felt himself starting to get excited as the teen spoke and drew his attention back to the show.

"Slow down, girl." The boy pushed her off him and looked around the area for something. The autumn sun had begun to dip into the horizon and the area under the bleachers was dimming.

"Why? You want me, don't you? Or do you want to play games? You want sex? Have sex. I'm sure as hell not going to stop you! But I'll play if you want…" She grinned and scrambled past him. "Catch me and you can have me."

The boy rolled his eyes and gave another cursory glance around before grabbing a handful of napkins from the dispenser under the counter.

Brittany laughed like a child getting away with something as she turned at the end of the bleachers and ran out to the field. "Plus, the grass is softer!"

The boy grinned like someone with a great idea they weren't sharing. He pulled his pants up and simply held them there as he chased her, frantically trying to shove the napkins into a front pocket.

Henry needed to follow. He knew that. He needed to be part of this now. They had brought it to him and his definition of lust was getting muddied with their own. He glanced around, unsure what he was looking for, but settled on the bucket and the short length of pipe he used to torque the missing handle on the water spigot. He grabbed the bucket by the handle and pulled the pipe free from his cart. He didn't have a plan, but he had an idea.

Henry slipped to the end of the bleachers and dared a look, as the boy caught up to the girl and dusk triggered the automated lights around the field meant to keep trespassers out—this pair didn't seem to notice. They tumbled to the ground as Henry moved up along the side of the rusted Ford and used its shadow for shelter.

The boy's mouth met Brittany's the same time his hand found the flesh of her thigh, his tongue pushing past her lips as his fingers pushed her skirt higher.

"No underwear?" Surprise evident in his eyes.

She answered with a smile and rolled on top of him, expertly slinking backward, away from his face, shimmying his pants down to his ankles on her way. Brittany raised an eyebrow at the no longer flaccid penis popping free of the denim, standing at attention like a soldier awaiting an order. She cupped his nuts, pulling them up enough to teasingly tap her index finger against the backside of his sack. She bent down and dragged her tongue along the scar-like line of his perineum. Against the laws of nature and the cool night air, Henry saw the boy's cock grew harder still, as he heard himself gasp. Covering his mouth, he waited, but they didn't stop. They hadn't heard him.

They didn't notice anything outside their own flesh.

Henry exhaled and squinted to get a better look. He watched with a slack jaw as the girl stroked the base of the thick vein raised on the front of the boy's penis. He watched her movements and compared his own body to that of the half naked boy on the field. He was enthralled with the boy's penis. He'd heard menstrual blood tasted different. But now he found himself wondering if blood from *that* vein would taste different than what he collected from the jugular.

She wrapped her lips around the boy for a brief moment, before she gave him a pouty look and released him. She flicked her tongue down at the base of his penis repeatedly, before she dragged it up the length of him. She was rewarded at the tip with a drop of pre-cum.

She moaned and Henry wondered if she watched porn to get ideas or if girls naturally knew how to make boys crazy. He'd logged onto a vampire-specific site once. There were videos, articles, and message boards full of curious humans and filthy vampires, as well as a few anonymous vampires who told tall tales of sex leading to death. He'd watched parts and pieces of a few of the videos, but found himself more interested in the articles and illegal retelling of murders. He had been excited during one video when a girl with pale skin and full lips had drawn a hint of blood with her teeth, but the culmination of the session hadn't done anything for him in the end. That was when he learned he was physically excited by things other than sex, and he began reading true accounts of vampirism instead—leaving porn sites behind for the anonymous message boards of 4chan.

He looked back to the sex on the field, twisted it to be what excited *him*, and wondered what the girl's blood would taste like. He'd only collected from men so far, and felt himself getting aroused at the idea. He watched her swirl her tongue around the head of the boy's throbbing penis, nonchalantly catching the glistening pre-cum as she went. She pointed her tongue and flicked it at the dimple on the head. Then she flattened her tongue and laved upward, before pointing it again and delving into the slit at the tip.

The boy groaned loudly. In response, she took him into her mouth as far as she could. The boy's breathing skipped, and as she slid back off him he pulled her down to the grass. Henry expected him to climb on top of her and ride her as they had in the videos, but he surprised Henry.

Instead, the boy's face disappeared between her thighs. She arched her back in response. The boy pulled away, looked at the girl and returned the same wicked smiled she'd given him earlier before delving his tongue into her core.

The moan that escaped her startled Henry, as did the sensation. He imagined her taste, seasoned with fresh blood.

After several minutes of his own daydreams overriding their pleasure, talking caused him to blink and focus back on them. Brittany had pushed his head away and he sat up, tilting her head at him like a confused puppy. "Why should you get all the fun?" She leaned forward, more flexible than Henry would have thought, and took him into her mouth again. Her eyes were focused on the cock in front of her. His head was lifted to the night sky but his eyes were closed.

Neither saw Henry stand up next to the truck.

As he stepped toward the couple, having decided he wanted to taste the girl, he froze when they changed positions.

Forcibly pushing Brittany down to the grass, the boy mounted her, declaring an end to foreplay with a grunt, the glint in his eye let her know his hunger had reached its limits. She pulled her legs up along his ribs and wrapped her arms around him, stretching her neck up to find his lips. As the tip of his cock teased her, sliding along her length and spreading her wetness as it moved, Henry slowly approached the unaware couple.

Their lustful hunger for orgasm had taken over, the boy thrust into her again and again. Her hips rose to meet him, as her lips reached upward to meld and move with his, before gasping and releasing his mouth in order to better control her breathing.

The hot lights of the football field and the cool night air were forgotten as sweat began to form along their skin, increasing the fluid-like slide of their bodies against each other. The crescendo continued to build as their breathing turned raspy. Her legs wrapped tighter around him as she rode the pleasure toward climax. She opened her eyes, intent on the boy's face.

But Henry saw it.

He watched her catch his blur of movement, as the pipe sliced through the air toward the boy's head. The boy fell limp, trapping the girl under his body, still connected at the groin. Henry rolled the boy off, as he raised the pipe for a second strike and smiled at the girl. *Brittany.* The slut he'd seen with so many boys.

Henry would be the last boy she saw.

She screamed. Her voice was lost in the acoustics of the field and bleachers, like so many cheering fans on game night. He put the bucket down and swung the pipe hard enough to knock her out. He didn't need the blow to kill. He knew the blood loss would.

SIXTEEN

Connor debated the differences between the files and the conversation he'd had with the coroner, both initially and *after* Rogers had taken time to look back at both cases. The detective talked to himself while he drove, trying to piece together some sort of profile on the killer—under the assumption they were both killed by the same person.

"Gotta be a guy," he reasoned, mumbling his assessment no woman would be able to overpower the first one, Winter. He had been a heavyset man who'd once had muscles, but at the time of his death, had been reduced to the forgotten bulk of age.

"Young. The lower end of the standard twenty-five to forty for serial killers." He spoke a little louder in the car, chewing over the case and profile as if someone were there with him to bounce his thoughts off. He glanced at the files on the front seat.

"White. *Definitely* white. And probably poor. Killing within his own comfort zone." He drummed his fingers on the steering wheel as he thought, pausing at the stop sign. He glanced at the football field as he started to turn the corner away from the park.

"Oh, Goddamnit." He hit the brakes and turned the wheel the opposite direction to head for the concession area and the pickup truck there. "Fucking kids."

As he approached the field, he gave the siren a flick, long enough for a single WHOOP to get the attention of whoever was in the truck. Pulling up behind the rusted

Ford Ranger, he turned his lights on with no noise. Allowing the blue and red to wash over the truck and its interior. He didn't need to see naked teens, so he gave them a minute.

When no one sat up, he looked around but saw no signs of movement anywhere outside the vehicle. He stepped out of his squad car and walked cautiously up alongside the truck, peering into the windows with his small but overly bright flashlight. No one. He turned and headed for the concession area. As he approached the overhang of the bleachers, he glanced back at the field.

"Oh *shit*."

He could see more red than turf in an area under the bright lights of the field. Even several yards away he could tell it was a mess of blood and flesh, clothes and hair. Connor grabbed his cell from his pocket and called for backup. The speed dial he had set up was for the station, not for dispatch, and the night captain picked up.

"Hey Richard, we got a situation at the ball field. Another death."

"Like the other two? Serial?" The night captain was technically a lieutenant, but on the after-hours shift he took on all the duties of a captain, including catching up on all active cases. Lieutenant Richards had literally gone over Connors cases with him no more than ten minutes ago.

In the background he could hear heckling from several of the night shift cops who were no better than the close-minded assholes he dealt with during the day. "Is that cereal with a C, 'cos they're eating it?" The snark was called out near Richards and the phone was muffled long enough for him to bark at someone before returning to Connor. "What are you looking at? Transient?"

"Got a pickup truck, so no. Hang on."

Detective Connor looked around for signs of activity, movement, a perp still in the area. Seeing nothing, he made his way toward the bloody swatch of field. As he closed in and the carnage became clearer, he felt the saliva in his mouth grow bitter and he held back a gag threatening to become vomit.

These are kids. Just kids. They can't be any older than Tamara. Jesus—

He looked at the red hair on the girl and swallowed hard. The color had brought the idea of facing his own daughter's death far too close to the surface, but he could see the girl was actually a blonde. The red wasn't her hair color, it was the blood—smeared over both their bodies, and spilled into the turf around them.

"Send an ambulance, body bags, forensics. Wake 'em *all* up, there's a mess out here." He could hear the panic in his voice.

The lights overhead illuminated the bodies, but he still swung his flashlight over them. It looked like most of the blood had come from the boy—lying on his back, staring at the night sky with a caved-in head and a ruined groin. In the chaos of muscle and flesh, Connor could see the kid's genitals were missing. He glanced at the ground. The blood was fresh. There were no tracks other than humanoid.

This was quick. In and out and run.

Eaten? Wild animals usually went for the soft tissue first—eyes, tongue, soft belly flesh that tears easily.

Unless it was a person.

There was still steam coming from the gore—*too fresh for someone to have sat here for long.*

Connor didn't believe the missing organs had been eaten on the field, but rather taken. *Maybe for food, maybe not. Maybe as a trophy.* Either way, they'd been removed *cruelly*, without skill or discipline, and were likely torn without a sharp object from the tears and destruction he could see in the flesh.

"Connor?"

"Yeah, sorry." He didn't know how many times the lieutenant had said his name.

"Is it the same guy?"

"I… I don't think so. This is fucking brutal. There are two kids. Hang on…" He knelt by the girl. No, this felt different.

He scanned the bodies, moving upward. The boy's groin had taken most of the damage, though a bloodied indent on the side of his head suggested he'd been killed first, rather than bled like the victims in his files.

The girl's skirt was pushed up to her waist. Her genitals were equally shredded, but there were also bite marks in the flesh of her upper thigh. Humanoid, not animal. The girl's shirt was torn in a manner that made it hard to tell if its removal had been during coitus, or in the mayhem of her murder. He saw more bite marks in the flesh on and near her left breast. Some were clean, as if the attacker had clamped down, biting hard enough to leave an impression and break the skin, but without doing too much damage. Others were torn, as if the bite was only to get a grip on the flesh in order to pull it away. Blood had dripped and dried at each of the attack sites—the bites on her breast, at a similar but less brutal bash to *her* head from what appeared to be the same weapon used on the boy, smeared around her torn vaginal flesh, and—

"Fuck."

There, in the matted mess of bloodied hair beginning to dry against the girl's neck, he saw it. Several tears and indiscriminate gouges, and a single puncture wound.

"Connor?"

"It's him." He stood and looked around the field. "It's him but something's wrong. Different tools? Something... It's him, but he's coming *unhinged*. This is different. Violent. Angry."

"I'm sending the teams. You'll get your task force."

"Hey, send me Bollard. He's not an ass like the rest of them, and the last thing we need is more live feeds of cops behaving badly on social media." He hung up and slipped the phone back in his pocket.

Connor had been the lead on *two* lamian murders in the last ten years. Both had been brutal and neither had been declared fully sane. Connor knew there were bad lamians out there—he'd seen their handiwork, both in person and on reports. But that didn't mean they were all bad. His father had always told him, "*Hate* the person, not a people." Of course, his mother usually followed up with, "*Hate* is an awfully strong word. Use it sparingly."

They were both right. But now, now we have hate crimes. Because it's not only an awful word, but an awful thing, and complacently commonplace.

He would need to get the chief to write a press release, stating this wasn't necessarily lamian. If he could convince him, he'd suggest he should point blank claim it *is* human, before the hateful took it upon themselves to spread their beliefs and cause panic.

More problems, more crimes, more hate.

Connor did another turn around the field, pointing his flashlight out at the perimeter and wishing it would shine farther. No movement, no motion, and no obvious perpetrator watching from the edges of his vision. He looked back down to the bodies and shuddered, positive in his assessment.

This guy is human. And he's escalating toward something awful.

─ SEVENTEEN ─

Friday morning, *Fox & Friends* wasn't on Andrea's television. They were *national*—covering big stories and famous people. Instead, Andrea was glued to the *local* news, as they covered the murders in town. *Her* town. The murders Andrea had been mostly unaware of until now. She'd known about one, late last week, but that was it. Just the one.

And now there were five?

She couldn't believe it was actually happening. *In Riverside.* A small town by big-city standards and a big town by small-town standards, Riverside was just large enough to have a wrong side of the tracks *and* a tourist district. Known for its annual duck race—hundreds of rubber ducks let loose in the river, picnics along its shores to watch, all in the name of community—Andrea dreaded the idea of her little burb being known for vampire murders instead of the innocence of rubber ducks. Riverside wouldn't be quaint and special anymore. It would be like every other dangerous place in the world.

Andrea felt somewhere between sick and sad, as she watched the local anchor team tell the story with a patented Ping-Pong exchange of information and questions.

"So you've been looking into this since the developments last night, right Tom? How was the first murder not considered a homicide until now?" The brunette's face had enough wrinkles for Andrea to question whether the shoulder length waves were her natural hair color.

"Apparently animals got into the house and there was some question about whether it was a *natural* death and simply an unfortunate aftermath with encroaching wildlife. Due to lack of family members, the victim, a Mr. Erwin Winter, was not discovered for several days, and his remains were a gruesome sight for officers and the truth of his death wasn't immediately known."

"And the most recent? The young lovers?" She'd been playing the anchor role long enough to almost sound uninformed, as if her questions were for herself rather than the audience tuned in for her acting.

Andrea saw through it and sneered at the theatrics. *Just get to the story.*

In response, the man who had been giving Riverside its news since Andrea could remember—and who would likely retire soon guessing from the new shake in his voice—nodded his head with tightly pinched lips.

"Yes. Seems a young couple, still in high school, according to our sources, was murdered last night at the school's football field. The information leaked so far includes rather disturbing, graphic images. But most confirmed details are still being withheld by officials." He turned from his partner and looked directly at the camera.

At Andrea.

"We also now know a young man, previously reported on last week, by the name Erik Smith, was part of this ongoing tragedy, as some key element has tied him to the others and he was apparently the one officials were working on when they began tying it all together. As well as a fifth body—which was actually found downstream by the Springfield Police Department and only this morning connected to our own situation. Whether that victim was killed before or after what they were referring to as the *first* case, is unclear at this time. People…" He blinked at the camera, and his face both softened with concern and intensified with a fear that could have been practiced or genuine but Andrea couldn't tell. "Citizens. Neighbors. Friends… It seems we have a killer loose on our streets. For more on what *you* should do, here is our own Bart Walder."

The camera cut to a man standing outside the police station, "Thanks, Tom. Officials aren't saying much, citing *fear of social retaliation* and *vigilante justice*, as well as claiming they're trying to avoid demonstrations and riots like other towns have endured after these *types* of crimes." He paused and raised an eyebrow. "These comments by officials make it *sound* like a lamian-based crime, and their actions and worries only further cement that presumption."

Andrea leaned forward, glued to his every word— spoken or implied.

"What we have ascertained for sure, is that each of these murders took place at night, and officials are now reminding citizens, we do not live in the golden age of neighborhood awareness, and to please remember to lock your doors and windows at night. Leave an outside light on if you will be coming, going, or expecting company, deliveries, or other known guests. And if you see *anything* at all suspicious, you should call the hotline here on your screen." The reporter pointed down, as if he could see the 800-number that popped up as he spoke. "The police are planning a news briefing at the courthouse in several hours. We'll get you more information then. Back to you, Tom."

"You heard him," the brunette started reiterating everything the other reporter had said, but Andrea drifted off, lost in thoughts.

They're killers. They've always been killers. They're not like us. They're dangerous.

Both sides of the argument had their own television stations, their own reporters, their own demonstrations and statistics which leaned conveniently the way they wanted, but what it came down to was the truth right there on her television. Five people dead in her little town because of *one of them.* She glanced up at the pictures on her wall. At her son.

He's dangerous.

He may not be a criminal yet, may not have killed anyone yet, but he will. They all do. And it will be my fault because I did nothing about it.

But what can I do?

Andrea's mind swirled with preemptive guilt, with shame for murders that hadn't happened yet. She imagined the funerals she'd have to attend so she could apologize to the families for her son's behavior. She would be ostracized at church, sermons would be directed right at her without Father Clark having to announce or admit it. She would know. *Everyone* would know.

I have to stop him.

The thought came so unexpectedly. She'd almost heard it in a foreign voice.

But how? He's too strong to take down. He's so much taller than me now. Maybe in his sleep, with a pillow? But if he wakes up, he'll overpower me and I'll be the next one on the news.

So deep in her own thoughts, Andrea didn't see Dillon come into the room behind her. She didn't see him freeze and cock his head at her. She didn't witness the blend of fear and disgust wash across his face before he quietly slipped back out of the room and up the stairs.

Andrea glanced at the pictures on the wall, the

snapshots of their life together so far, and paused at each one trying to remember if he'd shown any violence the day the picture had been taken. On *any* day. If *anyone* in her family had been violent, could he have inherited it from her side and the lamian genes from his father's side would tip him over the edge?

How do I stop him? She returned to the darker, more final, line of questions.

Maybe his food... Poison?

Her mind ran through various recipes she knew and a plethora of household chemicals, trying to find a combination to both hide the flavor of the poison and be something he enjoyed enough to guarantee he'd get seconds. To make sure he'd get enough of the poison.

Andrea snapped out of her murderous thoughts when she heard the door shut and glanced to the window. Dillon was off to school with his backpack bulging.

Strange, she thought. *He doesn't usually bother with a bag.*

EIGHTEEN

Madison hadn't taken a single note through biology class. She hadn't even heard the lecture. She was busy, frantically chewing at the fingernail on her index finger and trying to figure out what she was going to do.

The first tooth had fallen out. In its place, a tiny nub had already broken skin in the socket and was eagerly pushing its way through to fill the empty space. She'd spent the last two days covering her mouth when she laughed, moving her lips no more than a bad ventriloquist, and doing everything she could to mask the gaping hole in her mouth that would announce to everyone what she truly was. And now her second canine was more than a little loose.

This is happening. This is real. The two sentences rolled past her thoughts repeatedly, like a mantra of panic.

The sudden taste of blood pulled her back to the classroom and made her instantly nauseous. Madison almost spit without thinking. Instead, she held it in her mouth, gathered her things and walked out as fast as she could.

She didn't ask to be excused.

She didn't bother to grab a hall pass from the desk.

Once in the hall, she ran the short distance to the girls' bathroom. The janitor raised an eyebrow at her as she passed him, but she didn't take it to be any type of wet floor warning or other reason to slow down, so she kept going.

Madison burst through the door, dropping her things

by the closest sink and almost vomiting as she spat the blood into the porcelain bowl. She turned the water on and used her hand as a makeshift cup, bringing handfuls of water to her mouth to rinse and spit and repeat. When she could no longer taste the blood, she did it several more times in an attempt to rinse the memory of it away. Wiping her mouth with her hand, she looked at the mirror in horror.

What am I?

She pulled her lip up and looked at the nub of her new tooth, her tongue automatically flicking across its surface. The reflection reminded her of the source of blood and she saw the damage she'd done to her fingernail. She'd completely chewed off the loose part of the nail and part of the soft tissue beneath, leaving a red, raw, and now profusely bleeding stub with only a sliver of blue polish left at the very bottom of her nail.

She jumped as the bell went off and immediately let go of her lip—afraid someone would see her looking. They would know what she was inspecting. She turned her attention to the finger again and tried to ignore her mouth.

Madison flipped the water back on and put her finger under the stream, gently massaging the wound. She was trying to clean it without the shitty-smelling soap from the dispenser above the sink—convinced the pink liquid would sting in the open wound. She pulled away from the water to inspect the damage, grabbing a paper towel with her other hand.

The door opened and several girls entered, rushing to use the bathroom between classes. She ignored them, as they peripherally filed into the stalls behind her—chatting, phones beeping in response to texts, and dropping heavy backpacks with an almost rhythmic pattern of thuds.

"Ohhh… Better cover that before a vamp sees it and thinks it's snack time."

Madison heard Brenna's voice but didn't look up at her, afraid the other girl would see her fear. Instead, she played the part of snotty friend picking on lamians—as was expected of her.

"No shit, right? Got a Band-Aid in that mini suitcase of yours?"

"I think so." Brenna plopped her huge purse on the edge of the sink and rummaged through it. "What the hell did you do to your finger anyway? Looks like it's been chewed up by one of my mom's nasty little Chihuahuas."

"Nah, just me. Guess I hate this chapter of biology more than I thought." She grimaced, hearing the unintended dual meaning of her comment.

"Stings?"

Madison looked up at Brenna with confusion for a moment, wondering if her self-admonishing expression had been accompanied by a noise she didn't even notice.

"Hell of a face you're making." Brenna triumphantly pulled free a beat-up-looking bandage. "Here you go."

"Oh. Yeah. It stings. I chewed it way too low."

"Since when do you even chew on your nails? Gross. It looks like Rachel's hands. All nasty and ripped up. What the fuck, Maddie?"

"I don't fucking know. Okay, Brenna? Jeez. I wasn't thinking about it, I just did it." She took the Band-Aid from Brenna, braced for retaliation for her snapping at the more popular girl. None came.

Madison ripped open the Band-Aid wrapper and scoffed aloud when she saw it was covered in a flowered pattern.

Brenna smiled. "Hey, they don't make Band-Aids that actually match your skin color. And if you *gotta* show your wounds, at least make 'em pretty, right?"

"I guess." Madison had never thought about how pale a regular Band-Aid would look on Brenna's dark skin.

The second bell rang, announcing the beginning of the last class of the day.

"Shit, late." Madison grabbed her books and turned to the door.

"No worries. I heard we have a sub today for history." Brenna strolled without concern or speed out the door and down the hall.

Madison followed on autopilot, staring at her bandaged finger the entire time.

NINETEEN

Henry dumped the dirty rose-colored water from the bucket and squirted more generic dish soap into the bottom. Lavender fragrance drifted up and filled his nostrils for a moment, but the store brand soap wasn't strong enough to sustain the aroma—Henry could still smell the blood he'd carried home in the bucket. While he was normally excited by the heavy copper scent, this time he needed it to be gone. He shook his head and wished he had cleaned it right away rather than letting it sit overnight. But the high of the kill—the thrill that followed him home and ended in a night filled with two small glasses of fresh blood and the exploration of finger painting on his own skin with the coagulated lumps— had left him exhausted. Cleanup hadn't even occurred to him until this morning, and he hadn't had time to do it before he had to punch in at the school.

Now, even though the bucket had sat all day without soaking, he was surprised to find the dried blood itself flaked off fairly easy, but it left a distinct metallic smell different than the bucket itself. He couldn't return it to the school until he was sure. There hadn't even been much blood collected in it. But it was in the tiny creases and seam at the bottom, and the smell was as stubborn as a skunk on a curious dog.

He sprayed the hot water directly at the soap glob and let it foam up for a few seconds. Turning off the water, he reached for the bleach, uncapped it, poured some inside and then swirled it by moving the bucket in a circular motion. He set it down and dove in, scrubbing it again with the handled bristle brush reserved for dishes. At no point was he worried about reusing the brush on plates. It was hard enough to focus on the task at hand *physically* while his mind continued to wander back over the events.

He'd watched enough crime shows to know the police would think he'd taken a trophy, but it wasn't that. It wasn't about keeping something from the scene. To Henry, the boy's penis was simply holding blood he wanted to taste—nothing more than a *flesh* bucket. The metal one had held the girl's blood. And he'd been careful not to mix the two.

But the boy's hot blood... His thoughts wandered.

He'd been collecting the blood for later consumption, for fear of being interrupted at the scene. But he wasn't prepared for two victims, wasn't planning on *any* victims. And the spur-of-the-moment killing would have been wasted if he'd walked away with only *her* blood—the blood he was curious about, the blood he suddenly *needed*.

Before stabbing her neck with a screwdriver from the toolbox to collect her blood—his ice pick on the counter at home—Henry had bent over the boy and lapped eagerly at the blood from the head wound where he'd struck the youth with the pipe. He drank until it no longer ran free. He had forgotten how filling it was when still warm, fresh from the source. And he realized how much different it tasted than when it was reheated—like cold pepperoni pizza loses its zing, the blood loses a certain earthy taste.

But the boy may have been something else. It may have had something to do with the tissue leaking from the wound as well.

He'd then licked the bits from the pipe before turning to the girl.

On the way home, he'd thrown the pipe over the bridge. It was a scrap of forgotten garbage he'd rescued from the bleacher renovations the previous winter, and no one would tie it to him. It was construction trash. Nothing more. The screwdriver was one of many in his mismatched toolbox and would be neither missed nor tracked to him, and it went into the river as well.

The bucket, however, with the school name stenciled across it, came home with liquid treasure inside, and now required deep cleaning before returning it to work under their noses.

He could clearly remember the taste of the boy, and would find out if the blood in his penis tasted different on another day. It was the *girl's* blood, which had turned into a late night Henry could not have imagined.

It was sweeter. He was sure of it. It didn't have the same sharp copper flavor. It was smoother. The difference was as clear as when he'd splurged on a good bottle of whiskey just to taste the difference, after his grief swallowed up all of his mother's inherited half-empty bottles of bottom shelf labels.

There was *definitely* a difference. Both in whiskey and in blood.

At first he thought it was because she was a woman, different hormones hopping around her teenage body. But then, he remembered the young couple talking about her teeth.

Take them out.

Henry wondered if they had been completely fake, or if maybe they were placeholders for her new teeth to come in, a bridge or temporary denture of some sort. He cursed himself for not checking her teeth when he'd had the chance. He had no way of knowing if the blood tasted different because she was female, or lamian. And he had no idea how to target future victims until he knew this.

He grabbed a towel and wiped his hands without rinsing them—getting blood and bleach on the towel he knew he would throw away when he was done. He walked to the living room and turned the television on, then talked to his remote, "Local news."

Several options popped up on the screen and he chose the first one. It loaded the nightly program already in progress, mid-story. He pushed the button to start it over from the beginning, turned it up, and walked back to the kitchen. Back to scrubbing and remembering the previous night, he kept his attention loosely on the voices from the other room in hopes they'd talk about the murders.

His murders.

He'd heard the emotional gossiping and panic at school. He knew they were starting to tie his murders together and there had been some news story on that morning. But no one had even blinked at him today. No adults. No kids. And he was confident they had no idea it was him, or even human. He glanced at the counter where his keys were tossed, right next to the ice pick he used to pierce his victims' necks. It had started as wanting to be like them, to pierce the flesh like them, but it turns out, it might be good for them to think it's a lamian rather than human killer.

He was getting hungry thinking about the victims and the blood. He dumped and rinsed the bucket. Henry stuck his head right into the center and inhaled deeply. He smiled. It smelled like bleach. He put the bucket upside down in the dish rack.

I'll check again after it's dry.

He walked to the living room doorway and leaned against the jam, watching the talking heads banter back and forth about the things they deemed important enough to share with the public. An accident on the highway outside Springfield. Upcoming fall festivities. Unnaturally warm weather for October.

He watched the female anchor's mouth as she spoke. He wondered what *her* blood tasted like, and he knew he'd be taking another woman. He'd have to.

I have to know.

"On a national level, lawmakers are frantically trying to rationalize and regulate what they're calling hazardous waste, while a group of lamians are anonymously fighting to make it legal to *purchase* the biological byproducts of abortion clinics. The group states the clinic only *disposes* of the unwanted pregnancies, but they would gladly pay to take them, claiming it was no different than selling said waste to laboratories for stem cell research."

Henry blinked and looked up at the anchor's eyes.

What?

The screen changed to a clip of some senator from Pennsylvania shouting at the group. "To what end? Would you be purchasing these with the intent of packaging the tissue as snacks for *your kind* to buy? That directly breaches several clauses in the Stoker Treaty, and turns a deficiency, which can be dealt with as easily as diet or medication, into cannibalism. *Cannibalism under any circumstance is illegal in this country. In any civilized country.*" The senator looked both furious and disgusted, and the screen switched back to the anchor desk.

The anchor looked down to her papers and Henry thought about the ramifications.

The Japanese have plenty of strange things available in vending machines, why not tissue. We sell food for humans.

As if to answer his thoughts, the anchor continued.

"Likening such morsels to beef jerky, the group claimed to be bringing light and legality to a practice which is already prevalent among the black market deep on the Dark Web. Several special-agenda committees are looking into this atrocity and we'll have more as it develops." She flipped over a piece of paper.

Dark Web? A hidden Internet? Secret? How do I get there? How do I find it? Is it just a website? Where do I buy the bodies?

What do they taste like?

Are they clotted and cold like my samples, or are they preserved?

Henry looked at the bouncing screensaver of his computer and considered looking it up.

"Locally, we have no further information on the murders police are now collectively investigating as one case. A small task force has been created and they have been going back over each case to reexamine the scenes, bodies, and find links to help solve these.

"What we *do* know is they have been happening at *night* and officials are suggesting everyone stay inside after dark and lock your doors and windows. Those out during those hours should be prepared to be stopped and questioned.

"We are still waiting on all the names to be released—we know three men and two teens, a boy and a girl, have been killed and drained of their blood in the last several weeks. When pushed for details, an Officer Pettijohn said the killings are getting closer together, which is a sign the killer is beginning to unravel."

"I am not!" Henry stomped from the room, stopping in the middle of the kitchen with fists at his side, but still listening.

"While there is a pre-emptive tendency to blame lamians, the police department has confirmed at least one of the victims *was* lamian, and have urged the public not to believe this is any type of hate crime. Everyone is in danger, not only humans."

"*She* was the lamian." Henry spoke out loud, nodding to himself as his fists relaxed and a smile spread across his face.

The anchor's voice faded away against his own inner monologue.

It had to be her. Had to be. There was no reason to believe it had been any of the others.

So did she taste different because she was female, or because she was *lamian*? He'd need to kill one or the other to find out. The idea of killing caused his stomach to grumble. He'd gotten home and gone straight to work on the bucket. A glance outside showed him a twilight sky. Dinnertime.

He glanced at the recipes on the table and went to the fridge. The blood sausage he'd attempted was horrible, but he'd really enjoyed the Finnish dish called *blodplättar* from the weekend. *A blood pancake with orange juice.* He pushed the front jar to the side, the penis inside jostling against the glass in protest of the movement, and grabbed the last full jar of blood he had.

— TWENTY —

Dillon dropped his backpack on the ground and plopped onto the bench, slouching his shoulders with a heavy sigh. He had been wandering through town since school let out, which had turned into much more of a mental taxation than a physical one, but he felt tired, *weary*, nonetheless. He looked at the city park in the fading light of day and debated whether he could hide and sleep among the thick trees meant to mimic a wild forest.

The park was four city blocks, with a giant X-shaped path winding through it as if paved by a drunk. The path entered the park at each corner and eventually met in the middle. Each branch wound lazily through potted and planted floral and fauna, and various statuettes meticulously placed by the city beautification committee's blueprint. The center of the park was not only a junction, but meant to be paused at, enjoyed, with several benches and a fountain.

The fountain structure was about fifteen feet across with a short wall above the pool littered with pennies and a large statue of umbrellas at different heights against a thick ribbon of cement in the middle. The water bubbled up in four spots, strategically placed between each branch of the path, and sprinkled back down onto the umbrellas before running off into the pool again. Dillon knew they turned the fountain spouts off at dusk, but now he wondered if the water in the pool was clean water. *Drinkable* water.

He had taken two bottles of water from the house, along with a bag of chips, half a jar of peanut butter, and three small boxes of raisins. He discounted the pennies lying in the water and mentally totaled the cash in his pocket and the meager savings account built on birthday cards and Christmas gifts. He sighed. He didn't have much money, and his part-time job at Quikmart wasn't enough to live on.

The sun dipped farther and the decorative lampposts came to life throughout the park, triggering small circles of light and shutting off the waterspouts. The water suddenly stopping made the park seem even quieter than it had been. Almost too quiet. He thought he'd take the opportunity of silence to go through his options once more, trying to think of what he'd forgotten. Instead, a barrage of mental battering he couldn't escape sidetracked him. He considered his reality, as his internal berating refused to allow him enough of a break to focus on other things.

It wasn't that his mother was against lamians in general. She always had been. And it wasn't that she was a close-minded person with zero love in her for anything even romantically or incorrectly vampiric—*thank you, Hollywood*. Those feelings and opinions weren't new either. It was because he had actually *heard* her consider various ways to kill him.

Murder him.

He heard it clear as day. As if she'd been talking out loud. He hadn't imagined it. He hadn't unrealistically worried she *would* think that way, or presumed how she'd internalize the crap she was always watching on television. He'd been about to leave for school when it happened. When she'd considered his death, at her hands.

He had stopped. Frozen in place, as he initially picked

up her thoughts.

Maybe in his sleep… with a pillow.

She had thought those words. *His own mother.* He stayed still and stared at the back of her head, listening without meaning to, without wanting to, and heard her consider different ways to end him.

Backing up slowly, he'd retreated to his room, packed his favorite t-shirts and a change of jeans, slipped into the kitchen to raid what he could, and was out the back door while she sat there debating how to poison his food.

The teeth coming in had not been *unexpected* because of his father's DNA, but he had always hoped against it. If for no other reason than his mother's complete and unforgiving hatred of the lamians. When the gene made its existence known and his teeth came in, he'd started getting horrible headaches. He had attributed them to the stress of his mother's disappointment. Over the summer, the headaches gave way to an almost constant and annoying buzzing in his ear, like he'd been too close to an explosion and the ringing wouldn't go away. He'd brought it up to his mother, believing it was some condition he'd found on Google, but she'd never made the doctor's appointment. She had already moved beyond caring for him on a motherly level. The buzzing finally ended a couple weeks into the school year. It was replaced with an occasional word, in different voices, and before long, he realized he was picking up on things around him. He laughed at first and found it useless, referring to it as WKVR, the local underground radio station that was *never* quite in tune.

But now he was getting complete thoughts from others. He had not *read* her mind, so much as listened in while she talked to herself. While she convinced herself to kill him.

But why?

He wasn't a monster. He'd never hurt a fly. He'd never gotten in trouble for fighting or biting in preschool like other kids. *Nothing*. He'd done *nothing* to warrant her fear, and he certainly hadn't provoked her in any way big, little, or even enough to want him dead. Finding his father gone and hearing his mother wanted him dead, Dillon felt a loneliness in his chest that actually hurt as he wandered the streets. It hadn't lessened any by the time he revisited it all again on the park bench.

He ticked off his situation. He had a little money. Almost nothing to eat. Nowhere to sleep but the bushes behind him. *Unless I find an abandoned house down by the river, or maybe an unlocked car somewhere.* And he'd have to convince old man Mundy to give him more hours.

Dillon looked up at the sound of someone walking near the other side of the fountain, his view blocked by the huge umbrella statue. A young woman, girl maybe, it was hard to tell her age, rounded the fountain and came his direction.

Jesus, this kid's a wreck.

Hey, fuck you. He snapped at her mentally and furrowed his brows in response to her comment, emotionally pulling back from the stranger. *Who the hell are you to judge me.*

She stopped, cocked her head at him, and smiled.

Whoa, did I say that out loud? He was suddenly ashamed of himself for speaking to a stranger with foul language, let alone a young woman.

"Nah, you didn't say it out loud." She sat next to him and held a hand out. "Name's Victoria. Gimme a minute or two and I think I can help you."

He squinted his eyes at her and considered her bizarre offer, his situation, and the very obvious fact she had read his mind as easily as he'd read hers. *Lamian?*

"Yup. One of the good guys, though. Promise." She raised one eyebrow and bounced her hand in the air, as if to remind him of her extended offer.

He shook her hand. "Dillon."

"Had a rough few days, eh?" Her expression softened and he shrugged.

"Yeah. And it was kinda rude of you to listen in on my little breakdown." It was his turn to raise eyebrows, and he tilted his head forward to scold her actions without further words, much like a parent—like his mother—would, looking over glasses or through eyelashes.

"Sorry. I normally don't listen in on people. It's kind of a thing we agree not to do. But it was *really* loud."

"We?"

"*Polite* lamians, those who respect the privacy of others, and of course, anyone in the Lamplight Foundation. It's kind of a rule there."

"Lamplight?" He'd never heard of this and didn't even know if he could bother to care at the moment. He had other problems, bigger issues.

"It's an old…" She searched for the right word and finally settled on, "…club of lamians. Think *secret society*, since they were in hiding for so long—"

"What, like those Temple Knights?"

"Templar, but yeah, sure. Like that. Rather than fighting for anyone, they simply kept records. Really good records. Of *everything*. And now that lamians have been exposed, we're offering our knowledge and services more openly."

Dillon liked how she corrected him in passing, rather than making him feel dumb. And he liked her demeanor. She was friendly, and she put him at ease immediately. He'd never known anyone who could do that.

"So what can you *do* for me?" He only half-heartedly asked the question, as he looked her over and noted the little details making up her overall appearance.

She wasn't some thin, tight-clothed, heavy make-up, sexy, sultry being like Hollywood would have you believe all *vampires* are. Instead, she was almost plain. Not ugly, not at all. She had simple make-up, stylish hair, and appeared comfortable in her own skin—with soft curves that weren't pudgy but rather healthy. He could picture her in a dress as easily as a pair of jeans, and figured she'd look good in either.

Her blonde hair was very pale, washed out to the point of almost being white, but with enough yellow to be the color of lemonade. Her skin was a medium peach but not quite tan, like she had something other than northern Anglo in her bloodline, something quite opposite of the ancestors who gave her the pale hair. And her eyes. He stared at them while she spoke. They were almost *orange*.

"Well, for starters, we have bunks for visiting librarians and apprentices such as myself, so you don't need to sleep in the bushes here in the park. We also provide meals and transportation for those who need it." She smiled wide and exposed the tiny points of her canines, drawing his attention to them and remembering instantly she was like him, or rather, he was like her. "And they're technically brown."

"What?" He looked from her teeth back to her eyes in confusion.

"My eyes. They're technically brown. Yes, if you look closely, it almost seems like there's a ring of orange and a ring of green, right? But when you back up, they blend, and the DMV calls it brown."

He smiled sheepishly and wondered how much of his musing about her physical appearance she'd been listening to. He swallowed over the beginning lump of embarrassment and diverted the conversation back to the secret society.

"Food and shelter? Really? And what do I have to do?"

"Nothing. We're here to help. Honest." She held up her hand as if swearing on the Bible in court. "Our people go through some horrific times when the teeth come in. It's not the Dark Ages anymore, and we don't like to see people shunned, cast out, left to wander. So we shelter them until they…" Again, she chose her words. "Well, until they get their shit together." She smiled.

"Oh yeah?"

"Yeah. And no, I'm not talking about you. You seem pretty together, but like most who experience what you're going through, you're a minor. So we offer food and shelter, as well as teach you what you should know about yourself, and provide counseling to attempt reconciliation to those families torn apart by misunderstanding or prejudices."

"Ding ding, that would be me." His mouth twisted into a smirk to match his snarky tone of voice. "Sounds like a plan, until you meet my mother."

"That's a battle for another day. For today, let's get you back to the house and settled in. There's no one visiting right now, so you have your choice of rooms, and Max will want to talk to you."

"House?" Dillon watched her stand but didn't immediately follow suit. "Max?"

"Well, I call it a house. It was once. Or maybe a bed-and-breakfast? I don't know. It's freaking huge though. The downstairs is all library, with a kitchen tucked into the back and a small parlor we use for weekly meetings. The upstairs is studies, bathrooms, quarters, and—wait for it—a *free* bed." She smiled and held out a hand, offering to help him stand. "Come on, it's actually right around the block from the park."

"Wait. Right here? In town?" Dillon wondered how his mother hadn't been aware of this, knowing she would have completely freaked out at its existence.

"Right here. We've been right here for decades. We just don't jump up and down and announce it. Don't want to invite hate."

He nodded and stood without her assistance, swooping low to grab his backpack without ever taking his eyes off her. Her speech was too young, her word choices fresh.

She can't be more than twenty-five.

"Wrong." She turned and started to walk down the right path. "And only one of the many things we can teach you. We age to about twenty-two or so and then our appearance hangs right there for a couple decades. Then you'll age to fortyish and hang there. And so on. Remember, we live a *lot* longer. And *thank God* we don't spend the last half looking like we're a hundred. Although Max is starting to look his age."

— TWENTY-ONE —

Connor opened the cupboard and pulled out a metallic travel mug with a faded logo on it. He twisted the top off and set it on the counter as he grabbed the mug Jacqueline had filled for him, prepared to dump it in and leave.

"Really?" She knew his actions without words meant overtime at the station. The silence was his way of not bringing it up and having a fight about it. His plan was to slip out the door before she noticed. But he'd been noticed.

"I've got some things about this case bothering the hell out of me, hon. And I didn't sleep for shit. I'm going to meet with Rogers in the morgue and go over things. Maybe we'll figure out what I'm missing."

"You working on the murder that was on TV?" Tamara appeared in her pajamas. Her hair was a tangled mess that had been neat braids when she went to bed, and yesterday's mascara was smeared haphazardly.

"Um, yes." He hated talking about work with them.

"Murder?" Jacqueline looked between the two of them and furrowed her brows.

He put the travel mug down and sat with the full coffee cup in his hand. "Okay. But only because it may affect us."

"What?" Tamara's eyes widened as her mouth hung open in a circle of shock. "Wait, I need a Pop-Tart." She went to the corner cabinet and grabbed the entire box of strawberry Pop-Tarts. Retrieving a two-pack, she left the box on the counter and turned back to them. She tore open the packaging and bit the corner off one of the dry pastries inside.

"You know those are a million times better when toasted, with butter." He grimaced at her eating it raw.

"Yeah well, apparently it doesn't matter, it's useless to me in its lovely sugary carby state. Hey, I wonder if they make meat flavored?" She nodded at her mother with a mischievous look on her face, which suggested they look into the possibility.

"Gross." Jacqueline had been deflecting Tamara's black humor regarding their new menu plans all week. "Now hush, I want to hear what your father has to say."

Tamara rolled her eyes and took another bite.

"Connor? Affect us *how*?" The worry creased her brow and seemed to darken her eyes.

"Just that there's a murderer loose. That pretty much affects everyone in his territory." He tried to inform them without telling them anything not publicly reported already.

"A murderer loose? Okay, *that* doesn't sound like the thugs you normally hunt down. Even those who have killed are usually just *thugs with guns* to you. But that phrase? *Loose. That* sounds… ominous. What gives?"

Connor looked at his wife and daughter, pausing on Tamara long enough to get her to meet his gaze. "You cannot talk about this to anyone. Period. You'll throw off the investigation and could get people hurt. *Killed.*"

Tamara nodded, still chewing, her eyes once again wide but with a more serious undertone. She swallowed loudly.

"I know you usually avoid the news because of my job, but there have been several murders. And I think they're all connected."

"Several?" Jacqueline put her cup down and sat a little taller.

"Are these—" Tamara spit a couple crumbs and held up her hand while she finished chewing the bite and swallowed. "Are these vampire murders?" She reached across the table and grabbed her mother's coffee cup, taking a sip to wash down the Pop-Tart.

"Lamian." Jacqueline corrected her as she stood and retrieved a glass of milk for Tamara.

"No Mom, when they're murderous thugs, they're *vampires*. Just like white trash and every other horrible derogatory term is used when *earned*."

"No, Tam. They're lamian." Connor sided with Jacqueline. "No matter what they've done. And maybe this guy is. Maybe... Yes. But not likely. It looks like the perp is trying to make it *look* like teeth, and he's taking—" Connor stopped himself, they didn't need to know certain details.

"So it's a human trying to frame lamians? Seriously? How is that even a thing?" Tamara pulled the second Pop-Tart from the packaging, crumpled the wrapper, and tossed it across the table toward the garbage can. The wad unfurled itself, as the lightweight foil barely made it past the edge of the table and floated to the floor. She rolled her eyes at the missed basket but addressed her father. "Damn."

Jacqueline glanced sideways at her daughter before reaching down to retrieve the discarded wrapper. She dropped it in the trash, set the glass of milk in front of her daughter, and sat back down.

Connor spoke, as though the missed basketball try-outs in his kitchen hadn't distracted him. "Actually, I'm surprised it doesn't happen more often. The hate crimes are out of control in some areas of the world. Some cities in *this* country are actually downright dangerous for a lamian to try to visit, let alone live in. And why not fake something or frame lamians, right? If you truly hate someone or something, why not try and grow hatred in others, cultivate it, by *proving* your hate is warranted. They do it with fake news, social media drama, why not take it the next step and *prove* they're violent by killing people and pinning it on lamian?"

"That's seriously effed up, Dad."

"And hard to track down. But there's something to these victims. Something—"

"Which murders? All of them?"

"Yeah. The two men in their homes, two kids on the field, and…" Connor paused, swallowing the memory of the football field and hiding how much it had affected him by pretending to debate how much to tell them. "Maybe more. I don't know yet, *for sure*, which ones are truly tied together. Two for sure, probably four, and quite likely all five."

He knew in his head, the one Springfield had emailed over was part of the same case. *And fucking Pettijohn let it slip to the press.* But they didn't have proof yet. That's what he needed to check out.

The file had been sent over Thursday, and he immediately requested an exhumation. The judge had dismissed it as unnecessary, stating the cause of death had been misadventure, but said if they could show significant doubt he'd reconsider. And the chief had given him extra manpower based solely on him instinctively tying them all together. He *needed* to keep those extra officers. He might need more than the two of them. He needed to *stop* this guy.

Springfield's coroner was a woman who had been both a doctor and an FBI teacher before retiring to her civic position. She was meeting Connor and Rogers this morning to look over their cases, the bodies, to see if they could connect the dots. The Springfield case had been a Riverside resident. He'd only landed on their slab because the river had taken him downstream to their department. Two dead in their homes with clean puncture wounds, two dead kids but only one punctured in the neck with what looked like a different instrument, and a floater bagged and tagged downstream with wounds to the neck. All at night. All within a month. *Most* of them missing at least *some* blood, not quite *drained* like the news was reporting. Only the football player seemed to be handled differently. They *had* to be connected.

Tamara's voice broke through his thoughts and he looked up at her. "What?"

"I *knew* those kids. I mean, I didn't hang out with them or *like* them even, but I knew them. We had a whole assembly yesterday because of it. They brought in shrinks for the drama queens who were crying over kids they didn't even know. And we got lectured on staying in groups of two and not being out at night." She paused, her gaze seemed to be focused elsewhere. "The two of them were together on the football field and it didn't seem to do them *any* good. It didn't keep them safe."

"It was also nighttime," Connor pointed out. "But the suggestion is valid. Don't walk to and from school anymore, okay. Not until we catch this guy."

Tamara looked at her father with a sardonic twinkle in her eye and a thin know-it-all simper.

"I promise not to be late anymore." He sighed at her unspoken accusation. "And if I am, you stay *right there* and wait for me. Got it?"

Tamara nodded.

"Go, hon. Go to the station and stop this asshole."

Jacqueline's voice and expression were sincere.

Connor nodded and stood. "Thanks. I know you hate when I work on the weekends, but—"

"Yeah, but I hate being afraid even more." She stood up and kissed him. "Plus, now I get to demand you take us out to dinner to make up for it."

"Oh, Pizza Hut!" Tamara raised both hands as if she'd won something.

"That's not dinner, that's crap. Let's get our money's worth." Jacqueline winked at Connor.

"Fine. Call and make the reservations. I'll be back by six."

— TWENTY-TWO —

Henry drove past the old bed-and-breakfast slowly, looking for signs of activity. He'd learned it was a lamian facility when an article was posted in the Community section of the newspaper several years back, before he'd dropped out of school. The Lamplight Foundation—run by lamians—was meant to educate and house other, newer, naïve lamians. They didn't advertise, and he couldn't remember ever seeing anything about them after the article, but they were still there. Still keeping all their information, all their secrets, inside the old bed-and-breakfast.

Henry had attended the Monday meetings twice, eager to learn, to belong. But when they asked why he was there, they *knew* he wasn't one of them. He claimed he wanted to learn, but their questions made him nervous and he stopped going. He still sat outside on the occasional Monday, wishing he could be inside. Be part of them. Part of their history. And he drove by when he was mentally submersed in his obsession with becoming as close as he could to being a vampire.

He'd been twitching since his meal Friday. The news getting it wrong about his motives had angered him. It put him in a foul mood. All he could smell was the bleach from cleaning the bucket, rather than the lovely blood pancakes wafting through the kitchen. His mood soured his senses, and dinner had tasted bitter because of it.

He'd spent Saturday on the Internet looking into black market tissue and blood, and he'd been turned around several times trying to figure out the Dark Web. He started to get uneasy as he realized he was suddenly receiving ads surprisingly close to the things he had only spoken of, *to himself*, but not actually searched for online. His dead-end searches and sense of being watched only frustrated him, and he declared it a waste of time. He needed something more immediate.

He knew he'd have the blood from the boy's penis later in the day—afraid it would spoil inside the flesh if he waited too long. And then he was down to the half jar. He was upset about everything else and running low on blood—not a good combination for his mood.

He drove away from the mansion, noting there were only two cars in the parking area behind the building.

He drove through the town slowly, casually going under the speed limit down Main Street and watching everyone. The town was quiet, as most were either in church or still in bed. A couple of shop owners were visible, preparing for the day. Beyond the edge of the small shops was the strip mall with its empty lot and dark windows. Only a couple of the stores in Riverside were open on Sundays, and even those wouldn't open for another hour or so. The business district ended at a stoplight, and Henry paused, waiting for it to turn green.

To his left, the new elementary school, a daycare, a playground, and a church were easily seen from the intersection. Around them a smattering of older homes—those too stubborn to leave when the area became overpopulated with children. To the right he knew several more churches were nestled among the more residential side of town leading to the river.

The river.

The light turned green and he turned to the right. The left would be quiet, empty. The right would have people to watch, to want.

Older people sitting on their porches with their coffee watched him drive by, nodding occasionally from politeness rather than recognition. Younger people stared at their phones or talked to whoever was near them, paying him no mind at all. An occasional dog walker or early morning jogger did yet another loop on their known trek.

The Riverside High School lot was empty and the field silent—no sports practices were on Sundays—but both church lots were full. The bells rang as he drove by and he knew the 9 o'clock mass was about to begin at the huge, overstated Catholic church.

An old-model Saturn sat idling in the church parking lot, gentle plumes of exhaust rising in the October morning air. It was the same light blue color as the broken robin's egg Henry found the previous spring near his eaves. Inside, a woman with jet-black hair was clutching the steering wheel with her head tilted backwards. He slowed down and saw her mouth open wide for several moments, before she flopped her head forward into her hands. He looked around. The other cars were all empty. The doors to the church had closed. Here was a female by herself, as if she were a sacrifice to him.

But it's a church parking lot. In broad daylight. He shook his head at the fleeting notion.

Henry looked back to the road and drove past the churches and homes until he came to the curve at the edge of town where the river went under an old stone bridge covered in loose gravel. He pulled over. The excitement of even debating whether to kill the woman or not had been enough to quicken his pulse and awaken his hunger. He needed to calm down. Scouting was one thing, but getting caught for recklessness was something else.

The bridge spanned the Green River, recently renamed because its original name had been deemed derogatory to the natives of the area. It had originally been a covered wooden bridge, but was replaced with a stone version with short walls sometime before World War I. In the mid-seventies, steel beams had been sunk into the riverbed to reinforce the center, and an underbelly of grid work was meant to act as a net and keep it from collapsing. But the stones were beginning to crumble under the weight of more traffic than it had ever been intended to hold. And rather than rebuild, the city simply covered the bridge with loose gravel to hide the flakes of stone falling to the ground from the short walls on either side of the narrow overpass. Tourists and outsiders who didn't know the history drove over it without a care. Locals held their breath while crossing.

Beyond the bridge, the road continued on to several small but expensive developments before entering farm country and eventually leading to the highway. To the left, the river wrapped back around the northern end of town. To the right, it flowed away from Riverside and lazily meandered around large rock formations for several miles before circling the outskirts of Springfield. He looked at the river and remembered the first night he'd tasted blood. Right there on that bridge.

He'd been coming back from seeing a movie in Springfield. He couldn't even remember what the movie had been now—only that it hadn't been as good as the reviews made it out to be. He didn't see the jogger wearing the dark blue running suit. The jogger didn't hear him approaching due to his headphones, blaring whatever he was using for motivation to exercise. Henry had looked away for only a second. When he looked up, he was on the bridge, the jogger was in front of him, and there was nowhere to go. No way to swerve.

He slammed his brakes but it was too late, and the gravel made the car slide, almost hydroplaning, rather than come to a sharp stop.

He only clipped the jogger. The man didn't come up onto the hood, or slam into the window. Instead, he seemed to spin as if doing some crazy dance move and was flung into the old stone wall of the bridge. Surprisingly, the momentum didn't send him over the stones and into the water, but instead stopped him and he fell to the ground at the base of the wall. Henry heard the man hit through his open window and knew the truth before he ever got out of the car.

Worried for the man's safety, Henry jumped from the car to see if he could help. Running around the front, he slipped on the headphones that had been knocked free and went down, landing on the sharp gravel with both hands in an attempt to prevent his face from hitting the rocks.

The man was crumpled in the shadow of the short wall, a massive gash on his head from where he'd slammed into the stone barrier. His leg lay at an awkward angle and Henry presumed he had clipped the jogger's leg and hip with the car.

"Oh my God, are you okay?" Henry shook the man. "I'm so sorry. I didn't see you. I didn't know…"

He continued to shake the man, lowering his head to get a look at the man's face as his sentence trailed off. The man's eyes were open, unblinking, and he stared at something beyond Henry.

"Oh God… oh God, oh God, oh God." Henry scooted back like a crab on his hands and feet, the scrapes on his palms stung, as more gravel dragged across the open wounds. His mind spun, trying to grasp the repercussions.

Jail. No way I can survive in jail. I didn't even make it through high school.

"No, no, no. This can't be happening." He crawled back toward the man, feeling the pain in his hands but ignoring it as the least of his worries. He shook him again. The man's eyes had lost their shine and a single tear had fallen down his cheek.

Henry reached over and put his hand on the man's neck, hoping to feel a pulse. He had no idea what he was doing and simply mimicked what he'd seen done on television. He felt nothing. He moved his hands and tried using the tips of his fingers. He still felt nothing.

He felt his own throat to feel where the jugular should be, where he could feel his own racing pulse. It was up higher than he'd been trying and he put his hand back on the man's neck. Only two fingers this time, up high under the jawbone.

Nothing.

The man was dead. He'd killed him.

Henry's mouth dried in spite of his nervous swallowing, as he thought through his options.

"I need to call the police. If I call the police right away, it'll show I tried to do the right thing. That I'm not a bad person."

He withdrew his hand and started to reach for his phone. It wasn't on him. It was in the car. He stood and headed to the passenger door to retrieve his phone, absently licking the stickiness from his fingers.

Henry froze and looked at his hand in the glare of his headlights. His hand was covered in blood. Red that looked almost black in the dim light coated his hand as if he'd dipped it in paint, except for the clean streak he'd created with his tongue.

It wasn't gross.

It was… It was good.

"Perhaps I'm more lamian than my DNA claims." He smiled up at the dark sky as if telling the universe it had been wrong about him.

He brought his hand to his mouth and licked more of the jogger's blood from his fingers, sucking on each one as he cleaned them. And then he got an idea.

Opening the car door, he glanced at his phone in the center console but ignored it, instead turning his attention to the glove box.

What do I have in here?

A cracked CD case that didn't close correctly anymore, a tire gauge, the vehicle's manual, and a vent-style air freshener he'd forgotten all about. He considered the tire gauge for a moment while he contemplated his intentions. Could he really do this?

The man is already dead. No one knows who did it. The fish will destroy the body. Why not?

He felt the edge of the tire gauge and frowned.

Not even close to sharp enough.

He put the gauge back in the glove box and shut the compartment. Smiling, he reached over and pulled his keys from the ignition. The large old-fashioned key for the boiler room had jagged teeth that were much deeper than the other keys on the ring.

This will do.

Henry walked back to the jogger, trepidation and nervousness in his step. His lips tasted like excitement and fear, as he licked the dryness from them. He knelt down and looked at the man's eyes again. Still open. Still unblinking. Still dead.

He won't mind.

He found the man's jugular again and put the key

against it, trying to tear into the flesh. The makeshift weapon wasn't going to saw through flesh and tendons. He turned it to the point in anger and jabbed it into the man's neck. The trickle of blood that came out with the key brought a smile to Henry's face. He stabbed at the man's neck several more times until the blood ran more freely.

Henry bent down and drank from the leak he'd created. Enjoying the free-flowing blood as it washed across his tongue, Henry began to reconsider every argument he'd ever heard claiming lamians didn't drink blood. He questioned all those who claimed it was gross and not what they were.

They'd obviously never tried it.

When the blood all too quickly stopped running, Henry realized the heart was no longer pumping it through the small openings and began sucking. When he couldn't get anything else out of the wound, he considered opening a different vein.

Perhaps one of the larger ones in the leg?

But he couldn't be sure how long he'd been on the bridge. He wasn't sure how much longer he'd be alone. He wiped his mouth and stood up. Looking down the road both ways, he smiled. He was lamian. If in practice only, he was one of them.

He hoisted the jogger up and rolled him over the side of the stone bridge. In the darkness, he couldn't see him land. And he barely heard the splash over the excitement pounding in his heart.

Henry licked his lips as he sat in the car remembering that first time. It had only been five weeks, but it seemed so much longer. It had sent him on a path he didn't regret. He may have wished on occasion he'd been more careful— as the image of the two teenagers came to mind—but overall, he could live with himself.

He pulled away from the bridge and headed back to town. He was hungry. He needed to go home and get a snack. And figure out how he was going to get more blood.

Female blood, he reminded himself.

He needed to know why the girl on the football field had tasted so much better.

And if that woman is still sitting in her car, maybe I should consider it a gift from God after all.

— TWENTY-THREE —

The church bells had stopped. The doors were closed. Service had begun. But Andrea was busy screaming at God in the parking lot. She yelled again at the top of her lungs and held it for as long as her exhale could last. The back of her throat burned, her eyes stung, and her chest hurt.

She had no idea what to do about the monster she'd given birth to. She had raised him to be better than her. She had spent years teaching him morals and ethics, and not because some book told her to, but because she wanted him to be a good person. She had sacrificed for him—staying single to concentrate on him, working overtime to support him and get him anything he needed, anything he wanted. But it didn't matter. None of it mattered after his teeth came loose and the truth grew back in their place.

She closed her mouth and flopped forward, burying her face in her hands and letting the tears flow. *God is testing me.*

Andrea hadn't seen Dillon since Friday, but it wasn't unusual on the weekends. She always hoped it meant he'd made a friend and was off doing normal teenage things. Instead, he was usually in his room—playing his video games on the television she'd bought him for Christmas, doing things on his phone, or working on homework. He was a loner. And she blamed herself for that as well.

Maybe if I had dated. Maybe if I hadn't acted like a loner myself, he would have reached out to more people. She looked up at the church and thought of her friends inside, *likely wondering where I am. I can't take the full blame for him being a loner. I have friends. He knows it. Why doesn't he?*

She had dressed for church and was prepared for another normal Sunday with God and muffins, but then she watched the morning news and her heart skipped a beat.

I never see him after dinner. He goes to his room. Or does he? Is he going out at night, and I don't know about it? He's quiet. He's always been quiet. Andrea couldn't count the times he'd snuck up on her without meaning to and startled her.

Her thoughts twisted the news into some sort of logical path leading to her son. Her panic about him becoming a monster slowly grew into the conviction he already was one. That *he* was the one running around town killing people.

The church's stained glass had always looked beautiful to her, but this morning it appeared to have more red than she remembered, and the morning sun seemed to strike those panels specifically.

Blood. It looks like blood. God is showing me the blood that will be on my hands if I do nothing. But I cannot go inside His house. Not until I've succeeded in the mission He's given me.

She put the car in drive and slowly pulled out of the parking lot. She wasn't leaving God behind so much as she was avoiding her friends.

Abraham didn't ask others for help.

She wouldn't be meeting the girls for muffins and chitchat after Father Clark's sermon. She didn't have the strength or concentration to uphold the lies she had told the week before, and she had other, more pressing matters to deal with.

She had to murder her child.

Five people were dead. All killed at night, when Andrea never saw Dillon. All drained of blood, like a lamian would do, like Dillon would do. All the murders happened in Riverside, because Dillon didn't have his license yet to travel and kill elsewhere. *He hadn't even asked to take the test when he turned sixteen*, and when Andrea questioned that, he said lots of kids his age didn't drive yet. Too many things pointed to her son.

But she couldn't call the police. She couldn't turn him in and become the human mother of a lamian murderer. She couldn't be plastered all over the national news, embarrassed and blamed, questioned and accused. That's not what God would want. God wouldn't want others to punish her for her failings. He'd want her to punish herself. To make her His instrument and then live with the sacrifice of her child.

She drove past Ruby's knowing she wouldn't be there today and wondered what the choices of fresh cookies were for the after church crowd. Then she chided herself and pulled into the parking lot of the hardware store.

It's not time to consider treats.

I need to be the hand of God. For He has given me a test and a duty.

Andrea had briefly looked online, using the older-model desktop computer she refused to update. Over-the-counter medications would take too much or too long. Rat poison would be much quicker, more effective. She'd put it in the taco meat for their traditional Tuesday meal and he'd never notice—not with the amount of hot sauce he usually added to his plate. He'd get sick for a few days and then he'd be gone. It would be over. He didn't have friends to miss him and she could claim he'd run away. The only part she hadn't worked out was what to do with his body.

She turned the car off, glancing at the time on the radio before pulling the keys. The sign on the door indicated the store would open in fifteen minutes. She could wait.

Patience is a virtue, she thought, but couldn't remember if the phrase had been in the Bible or if the quote had come from somewhere else.

Tuesday. It will all be done Tuesday. Once he's sick, he won't go out and kill anymore. He won't hurt anyone anymore. Suddenly she looked up and caught her reflection in the rearview mirror. *Tuesday? That's two more nights for him to attack. What if he finally comes for me?*

She watched her reflection without seeing it, as she imagined her bedroom and the furniture in it. She had a large wooden chest she could put in front of the door, or perhaps wedge the dressing chair under the knob. And the newscaster had said to lock the windows, so she'd need to buy a floor fan and shut her bedroom window at night. She needed to make sure he couldn't get to her after the sun went down.

She'd have to protect herself until Tuesday.

Until she could do something about Dillon. Her son. The monster she'd created.

TWENTY-FOUR

"Yes, while the witch hunts carried a certain, *similar* hysteria, at the heart of the matter they were chasing smoke. There was no such thing. On the other hand, lamians are very much real." Mrs. Fidler smiled at several students and Tamara wondered if it was because *they* were lamians, or because those students were humans who needed to pay attention to this lesson in particular.

"What about God then?" The boy at the front of the class talked without raising his hand. Tamara didn't remember his name, but she knew he'd been homeschooled his whole life until this year. Apparently all homeschooled kids were now required to attend at least one year in public school for their grades to count toward college. She figured he wasn't used to classroom etiquette.

"What about God?" Mrs. Fidler's look was one of pure curiosity. "We're discussing the social problems to consider for the report and how current events can be compared to previous causes and cases of cultural upheaval. God is theological, not cultural."

"Well, according to my mother, who is a full-blood— *both* her parents were lamian—the humans *stole* God from *us*." He said the part about his parents with a certain snotty pride.

Mrs. Fidler tilted her head like a confused dog for a moment, the smooth skin of her forehead barely wrinkling in response to the single raised eyebrow.

Tamara tried to figure out how old her teacher was. Younger than her parents, she figured—probably between the two. Mid-thirties maybe. She wondered if Mrs. Fidler had gone to this same school and was taught by some of the older teachers.

How weird would it be to be co-workers with your ex-math teacher?

Mrs. Fidler backed up into her desk and leaned against it. As she crossed her arms in front of her, a slow smile spread across her lips. "Okay, I'm listening. What, *in God's name*, are you talking about?"

Several snickers rippled through the class.

"My mother says the humans stole God and rewrote the Bible, taking us out of it. She says Adam and Eve were lamian, and they ate the forbidden fruit so God punished them by making fruit useless to them, forcing them to live on meat only. And not for nothing, but doesn't *that* make more sense than making girls bleed every month just because you ate an apple?"

Several boys murmured to each other and Mrs. Fidler flashed a silent warning.

"I don't think that was the extent of the human punishment. I'm not a big church goer, but I believe it was kicking them out of paradise and making their lives difficult in general."

"Still, does it make sense? Just because they ate a piece of fruit?"

"It's an interesting point. Perhaps I'll make *that* discussion its own assignment." Several students groaned and Tamara knew the kid had made a couple new enemies. "But let's get back on track for *this* assignment, okay?" She turned to the board and glanced at her bullet points there.

"Much like we used to teach about Martin Luther King Jr. annually, I'm sure you're all getting sick of this unit each year. But this is the last time. This is the year you write the big scary paper about it and move on. So, let's talk about the difference between prejudice and bigotry, before we move into how those opinions affect things."

"Why are we even still having a problem with them? Why is this still something to discuss? Or teach? Can't people just be nice to each other?" The girl to Tamara's left asked. *Stacy? Maybe?* Tamara couldn't remember her name, only that she asked enough questions to sound like a brown-nosed teacher's pet in every class she'd ever shared with her.

"That's a good question, isn't it? The lamians have been known and public for fifty years. The Treaty was passed for civil and social behavior, expectations, laws, etc. over twenty years ago. So why *are we* still hearing about hate crimes? Why do we still have to correct people and tell them not to call them vampires?" Mrs. Fidler looked around the room—her gaze landed on Dillon.

He shrugged.

"Anyone?" She looked up from him and waited. "Fear. The reason is fear."

"Mrs. Fidler, that doesn't make sense." The little brown-nose girl provided the pivot point to the teacher's argument as if it had been rehearsed.

"People fear what they don't understand, Tracy. *All* actions, from *anyone*, come down to one of two things: fear or love. Those who have never met a lamian base all their beliefs on what they're told, what they read, or what they see. If they are taught to be loving and respectful, then they view them a certain way. If what they are exposed to is toxic and negative, and they never meet one to counteract those teachings, how are they to believe otherwise? And then they have children and pass along incorrect information."

The teacher looked back to the homeschooled lamian.

"Much like religion is passed down from parent to child, so are opinions and prejudices. If your parents are overly *for* or *against* something, you tend to be as well. Politics often work the same way, as children usually become card-carrying members of whatever party their parents vote for—though sometimes they will flip to the other side as a show of protest as young adults."

She stood up and walked around the desk to the board. Tapping on each of the lines there, she continued. "It's the little things that change a big thing. For instance, take the first part of the problem path: OPINIONS. If we could form opinions based on experience rather than assumptions, we could solve many social problems. Prejudices are *pre*-judgments, as the word suggests, and not based on fact. Bigotry, on the other hand, is a stubborn will to hate. They may have all the truths, facts, and details, but they *choose* to be or stay intolerant to those who are different than them—whether it be color, sex, or as in this case, species."

She paused a beat to scan expressions. Tamara knew from experience she'd stop and backtrack if anyone looked lost. "Another thing that falls under these trigger words—and the umbrella of opinion—is when you lump people in collective groups of supposed fact. A derogatory connotation almost always happens along the way. *All men* are pigs. Or *all blondes* are dumb. Neither of these is true. But opinion is something people cling to, fiercely, protectively, as if it were their own tangible property and they can't let go of it. That is the core of bigotry and prejudice. And something as small as language can uphold an opinion... Or change it."

"So when my uncle calls people *hicks*, it's not just that they're from the country?" A confused looking boy near the front of the class cocked his head in thought.

"No. There's a full derogatory definition behind that word, and while it may change subtly from region to region, *hick* never means an educated, classy person. It almost always comes with the modifier *dumb*, whether it's spoken or not."

"But people don't have rallies for people to stop saying *hick*," the boy continued.

"No. But there are also no *hick* hate crimes. It's a derogatory term we shouldn't use, but it doesn't create social strife."

"Cuz they're too dumb to know it's mean." Tamara heard Amber whisper to Madison, and rolled her eyes at the Brenna-wannabe.

Mrs. Fidler seemed to hear it as well, as she continued with sharpness to her tone. "Unlike *vampire.* If everyone could make the effort to stop calling them *vampires*, even the bad ones, even in jest, or even in what some would call art—like the popular bands right now. The music from California is all gothic romantic Hollywood *vampires*, while the music in New York is heavily derogatory to lamians but claiming to do it from the inside, so it's okay if they call *each other* vampire. But no, it's not. Doing so only furthers the use of a word we've all agreed is degrading."

She looked at the back of the class in general, not stopping on any one student. "It's the small things, like the way you look at someone once you find out they're a lamian. Does that look come with a judgment of sorts? Did you mean it to? Will they take it that way even if you don't mean it that way? *Resting Bitch Face* causes enough problems in an overly sensitive society. Add the lamian element to a young person going through the changes, and they become highly sensitive to how they're perceived by those around them. You need to be aware of your words and actions. Not only should you not *fang-shame*, but you shouldn't take advantage of them or their plight."

"Like that company who's getting sued for those banned t-shirts?"

Tamara didn't bother to look around and find the source of the question, as she zoned out contemplating the list on the board. OPINIONS. CAUSES. PROTESTS. CRIMES. The last bullet point held her attention and she drifted off to think about the things her dad had told her about the murders, the lesson being heard but not paid attention to fully.

"Exactly. Sure they thought it was funny, but it was offensive to some." Mrs. Fidler caught someone's gaze and stopped. "For those who don't know what Terry is talking about, there was a t-shirt being sold that said MTGA on the front and on the back it said Making Transylvania Great Again. It was meant to be a proud way to show support for your lamian friends, but Transylvania having anything to do with lamians is a Hollywood derivative and *not true*, thus the t-shirt was simply furthering lies and hurting the cause rather than helping it. And making a profit doing so."

The room was silent for a moment as the teacher's words sunk in. The quiet was enough to snap Tamara free and she glanced around, noting who looked pensive and who looked annoyed.

"You should be aware of your words, your actions. You never know who around you, even in this class, is a lamian and hasn't come out yet."

Tamara saw Dillon nod her way, like a secret handshake acknowledging they knew about each other. She noticed several students watching their exchange, but then saw Madison and frowned. Her face was full of panic, and several of her fingers were tipped with Band-Aids.

What the hell, Maddie?

TWENTY-FIVE

Dillon stood outside the counselor's office door and thought about the assignment for Mrs. Fidler's class. He was seriously considering whether he should write the paper about his mother.

After all, she fit both the irrational pre-*judgment of a prejudicial person,* and *clung to her incorrect beliefs—even feeding them with the news she chose to watch—and thus was a willing bigot.*

The more Mrs. Fidler had talked about the assignment, or rather the social issues the assignment was about, the more upset Dillon had become. His *mother* was the embodiment of every single thing wrong with the country, *the world,* when it came to lamians. He wasn't better or worse than a human. He was just different. He shouldn't be judged because of his teeth, but because of his merits, his talents, his achievements.

I'm a good kid.

The self-affirmation wasn't something he thought often, but he knew it was the truth when he heard it in his mind. He worked hard at school and his part time job, did his chores without problems, and was always willing to help out when needed.

And I'm smart.

He wasn't the valedictorian or class president, but he was in the top ten students at the school and had more than enough awards, papers, and several scholarship leads for college already. He wasn't trash just because he was lamian.

My teeth don't negate my talents, my hard work.

And it suddenly pissed him off on a new level.

Fuck her.

Max had said he could stay with the Lamplight Foundation as long as he needed. But Max and Victoria believed they would be helping *fix* the rift between him and his mother. They thought they were sheltering him until he could go home. Dillon knew he wasn't ever going home. His mother was more than just an angry, judgmental human with unwarranted hatred toward lamians. She'd become a bigot with murderous intentions, and he wanted nothing to do with her.

But he was a minor. Technically, if she truly wanted, she could *force* him to return home.

Unless I emancipate myself from her.

He stared at the floor for a moment.

Or tell the judge she's a threat to me and request the Foundation take custody until February. I mean, I'll be eighteen in four months. It can't be that big of a deal, right?

Frustrated at the situation, he leaned back against the wall of lockers outside the counselor's office and flopped his head backward to stare at the ceiling. The tiles were still white and fresh looking. A huge renovation the previous summer to remove every last tiny trace of asbestos from the building had meant replacing ceiling tiles, insulation around some pipes, and something else Dillon couldn't recall. But he remembered the traffic around the school was completely jacked up all summer and the jocks were all a flutter because they had to practice at the public field rather than their own turf. *Wah wah,* Dillon mentally mimicked a baby crying.

He bounced his head lightly against the wall several times, the metallic thud a soundtrack for his frustration. He sighed and moved his head back down to a normal position and watched the stream of students. They moved either direction in the hallway, and he found if he didn't purposely focus on any of them in particular, he could pick up bits and pieces of thoughts.

He didn't like it. It sounded like a crazy person whispering behind him. Saying things that made no sense. Sentences that didn't connect. In voices that were never the same. It hurt his head and started to blend together into an incoherent buzz as if they were all talking at once, over each other, in a droning tone.

All he had to do to stop it was focus. Which he was pretty sure was the opposite of how it would work once he got the hang of it, but for now, by concentrating on one person, he could make the rest stop. Of course, he couldn't know for sure if what he may or may not pick up was actually coming from the person he focused on, or from someone nearby. Some with *stronger vibes*, as Victoria had explained to him.

Dillon saw Madison Hayward exit the bathroom and head his way. They'd been fringe acquaintances through most of their school years, always in the same advanced classes together but never once being paired for a partner project. He'd always thought she was pretty, but avoided her because she was tight with *the beast*.

Brenna had been Dillon's cubby partner in kindergarten and had been completely awful to him. She picked on his clothes, his lunch, even his hair—calling it greasy and stringy, compared to her tight natural curls and the bounce she considered adorable. She snorted at his answers and scoffed at his questions. His mother had tried to suggest she probably liked him. He couldn't fathom it and considered her a beast. Over the years, he'd watched as she matured into a full-on *bitch,* in his opinion. He couldn't stand her attitude, and the sound of her voice was enough to make him walk the opposite direction. But she wasn't with Madison at the moment, so he dared a fleeting glimpse and smiled at her, as she got closer.

He thought he'd picked up some of her thoughts in Study Hall. He thought she might be at least *interested* in lamian, if not hiding her truth from Brenna. He was intrigued either way, and still found her really cute. His smile was nervous and crooked, his eyes full of questions, and he swallowed over a lump as she got near.

But when they made eye contact what he saw was a flash of panic in Madison's eyes, but caught no inner thoughts at all. Nothing. From her or anyone near by, as if a barrier had been thrown up and silence descended.

She immediately put her head down and sped up. Not simply ignoring his silent hello, but running away from it.

What gives?

He had no time to consider what could be going on with Madison, as the counselor's door finally opened.

A kid Dillon knew only as Jake followed a teary-eyed woman out of the room. Dillon wasn't sure if he couldn't remember the kid's last name or had never known it. What he did know was the boy had been in trouble *repeatedly* over the years. He was in almost *all* the fights on and off school property. He'd gotten in trouble for bringing both a snake and a knife to school, on two *separate* occasions. He had started a fire in the boy's locker room, which had earned him a two-week suspension. And then there was eighth grade, where he disappeared for most of the year.

The rumor mill said Jake had been locked up in a psych ward, but Dillon thought it more likely he'd been sent to the local detention hall for private schooling and an attitude readjustment. Whatever the case was, he'd been gone for a while before eventually returning, having learned no lessons, and his troubled ways continued to get him sent to the office.

Jake turned and leered at Dillon, curling his lip up high so Dillon could see the still-growing new teeth Jake sprouted. The sneer had almost looked like a dare, or a warning, and made Dillon very uncomfortable. If Jake was lamian, there was a good chance he was going to turn out like every horrible stereotype claimed he would. Just like Dillon's mother would expect both of them to be.

The counselor's voice pulled Dillon's attention back to the doorway.

"Mr. Hubbard?" The counselor watched Jake and his mother walk away and rolled his eyes back toward Dillon. He sighed heavily. "First things first, is this about vampires?" The annoyance in the man's voice was aimed at the world at large, but landed squarely on Dillon's already fragile ego.

"Lamians, asshole. And *never mind*." Dillon spat his disgust at the man and walked away.

TWENTY-SIX

Madison was finishing up the dinner dishes when she jumped at the knock on the back door. She glanced into the living room but heard no response from her parents, and decided they likely didn't even hear it over the television program they were watching. The back door was reserved for friends and neighbors, neither of which was expected on a Monday night.

She had only nibbled at her dinner, her stomach and mind still arguing about what she should and shouldn't eat. Her mother noticed, and she made Madison sit there until her plate was empty. Madison had forced the last few bits of food down with a tear in her eye and hurriedly cleaned up so she could go hide in her room. But first, she apparently had to be pleasant to someone at the door.

She wiped her hands and eyes on the towel and hung it over the bar of the stove. Turning to the door, she announced her intentions loud enough for her parents to hear.

"I got it!"

Madison pulled the door open, expecting to see Mrs. Stanley from across the alley in need of milk or sugar, which was usually an excuse to gossip with Madison's mother. As the kitchen light washed over the guest on the doormat, Madison froze for a moment.

"Tamara? What are you doing here?"

"I thought maybe we should talk." Tamara smiled at her, like an old friend finally coming home.

"About what?" Madison mentally ran through her

day at school, trying to figure out what could have landed her ex-friend on her back porch.

"Your teeth." Tamara's eyes twinkled as she spilled the secret with a smirk.

"Oh my God, shhhh." Madison scooted outside and pulled the door shut behind her. "What's wrong with you?" She whispered in a scolding tone.

"Me?" Tamara pointed to the door. "What was *that* all about?"

"Are you crazy? They might hear you."

"Why—" Tamara started to question, but quickly realized what was going on as her confusion turned to revelation. "Wait, they don't know? Why not?"

"Because I'll get shunned—from school, from family. I'll become the girl who had a perfectly normal family and then her teeth came in and ruined everything. And I don't want that. I don't want them to be afraid I'm going to eat them, or God forbid actually think I might."

Tamara's eyes widened for a moment and then she doubled over with laughter. She laughed with a boisterous exaggeration and slapped her thigh as she stood back up. "Oh my God…" She covered her mouth and laughed some more. "You're completely serious, aren't you?"

Madison watched her friend's reaction and burst into tears. Every fear ran free in salty streams down her face.

"Oh my God, Maddie. Noooo…" Tamara stood upright and pulled her friend into her arms. Madison cried while Tamara shooed her softly.

"You don't have to be afraid, honey. Your mom and dad are cool. They've never been anything but tolerant. Why would you think they'd be different because it's you?"

"Because it's *me*."

"Oh silly. No. God, no." Tamara pulled Madison

down toward the step. "Come on, sit down. Talk to me. What the hell, Maddie? Let's start with those fingers. What did you do?"

"Just chewing my nails until they bleed. Which is gross by the way. Blood is gross, I don't want to drink blood."

Tamara snickered, holding back another big belly laugh. "You don't have to, silly. Change your diet, get the pills, there are things you can do. But you never, ever, *have* to drink blood. Cuz you're right. That's gross."

"But…" Madison looked up at her friend's calm face. The smile she'd known since kindergarten wasn't condescending or poking fun. It was genuinely sweet. Just like Tamara had always been.

"Honey, did you *used* to want to murder people?"

"No."

"Then why would you now? It doesn't change who you are on the inside, just what kind of nutrition you need. You're still good or bad based on *you*, your upbringing, your insides, your heart and soul. Jesus, ya big goofball. Why didn't you tell me?" Her eyes widened suddenly. "Oh my God, *Brenna*? Brenna doesn't know either, right?"

"Oh no. No, no, no." Fear washed over Madison's face.

"Doesn't matter. She'll push you away and that's fine. Eventually it will only be her and Tristan anyway. I'm here. Right here. Always have been."

"Really? That simple?"

"Yeah. And you should probably tell your parents sooner rather than later. You want me to come in, be with you? Do they know Brenna pushed me away? How'd they feel about that?"

"Honestly, my mom called her a bitch."

Tamara laughed. "Yeah well, even her closest friends

call her that."

"But how did you…" Madison's tears started again, more in relief than fear this time.

"How'd I what? Find out? My tooth came loose and I told my parents. Why wouldn't I? And—" Tamara's mouth hung open for a moment. "Oh God, that's right, you don't even *know*."

Madison shrugged, silently confirming her lack of knowledge and motioning for Tamara to continue.

"So it turns out my *mom* is lamian, basically a full-blood, and didn't know. First of all, she was adopted, can you believe that? They kept that from her. And *then*, when her tooth came loose they brought her to an orthodontist who specialized in hiding the truth. I mean, I can't even, right? This guy put on braces she didn't need, and pulled teeth claiming extra teeth, and something about movement and all kinds of things my dumb mom believed, cuz he was a *dentist*. Here it turns out he was paid to lie and make her believe it all. Apparently this was a thing back then. Can you imagine?"

Madison nodded. "Actually, yeah. I can. Considering the things I've been looking up lately and ways I've been debating hiding this."

"Why? It doesn't make you a monster anymore than it makes me one." Tamara cocked her head at Madison. "Do you think I'm a monster?"

Madison shook her head.

"I'm the opposite. I'm a friend. *Annnd*, we get to be friends for a damn long time now, cuz we're gonna live until almost two hundred." The excitement in Tamara's voice lifted the pitch and tone to that of an overly sugared child.

"Two hundred? What do you mean?"

"Oh there's so much you don't know." Tamara hugged

Madison again, releasing her with a giggle. "For someone who's in all the honors classes, you sure are stupid about this. You're gonna live a long time. Hell, didn't you hear about the first lamian judge who was nominated to the Supreme Court? That's a *lifetime* post, so now they're debating if they should change it because of the lifespan difference. You can be anything you want. And if you really want, you can be a monster. But I think you'll probably just be a big math nerd like you already are. Come on. There's a support group on Monday nights. Mom isn't going with me this week, but you are. Wait until you see this place, books that go back hundreds of years. Your inner nerd will freak out in that place. And the people, the lamians who run it, are super nice. You'll learn what you truly are, and then we'll tell your parents."

Tamara's excitement was infectious and Madison felt her worries lifting as her smile widened.

"I missed you, Tam."

"I never left."

TWENTY-SEVEN

Henry turned off the headlights and let the car coast to a stop along the road near the old slipway. With the new updated boat landing, complete with docks and crank-operated launches, no one used the old dirt trail that led to the river for putting smaller craft in and out of the water. Instead, it had become a forgotten parking area, the perfect lover's lane. And he was hoping someone was feeling feisty tonight. Looking for preoccupied people behind steamed-up windows of a car, not paying attention to him as he approached.

He shut the car door with only the whisper of a *click* and walked up to the dirt road opening leading to the river. Disappointment was the only thing waiting for him.

"Damn it."

He'd eaten a meal of boxed lasagna with regular red sauce on it, since he was currently *out* of his favorite ingredient—the Mason jars all sitting empty and clean on the edge of the sink as if to tease him. Desperate, determined, he had hopped on his computer and logged into Facebook after dinner.

He loved how trusting people were on social media sites. Even without *friends* in real life, he had plenty of *friends* online. All he'd had to do was join a couple of local groups and then start accepting their *friend requests* as they blindly welcomed him into their lives. He watched, as they told him exactly where they were, what they were doing, and even what they were eating. He knew who was married, who had kids, and thanks to the new profile specifications, whether they were lamian or human. Henry knew who he suspected was pretending life was great, and who was openly depressed, simply by viewing the pictures they shared and the memes they posted. He knew when they were home or out, alone or with friends.

Facebook was a stalker's dream.

But using it that way took time. And after checking the profiles of several of the women in his Riverside Yard Sale group, he grew restless. They were mostly married—all either home with family, or simply not disclosing their location tonight.

He wanted to find a female. He was out of blood. He *needed* the blood, but he *wanted* another female. The desire to figure out why the girl on the football field had tasted so much better, whether it was due to female hormones or lamian DNA, had become an obsession.

He thought he could log onto Facebook and shop as simply as if he were on Amazon's website. But it wasn't as easy as that, and the group was only making him agitated, as if they were teasing him on purpose. He needed to do something, to act on his desire, instead of cruising profiles and surfing the Internet. So he got in the car.

Henry sat in the driveway for several minutes, trying to figure out where to go. He tried to think of places where he could find women. He drove through the grocery store parking lot, slowly, hoping for a nighttime shopper to be away from her car, her purse, her phone—maybe putting a cart away in the corral where she could be easily overtaken. But no one was in the lot as he drove through, and he knew doing too many passes through the aisles would look suspicious.

He cruised past the Laundromat, only to find the lights off. He was more surprised at their early hours than at his assumption only *women* would be washing their clothes in the coin-operated machines.

The idea to drive down to the old boat landing seemed perfect, but turned out to be another disappointment. And now he was back in his car. He gripped the steering wheel with frustration, as he headed back into town.

He turned the corner by the closed hardware store and saw two girls coming out of the doorway that led to the apartment above the shops. *Two* girls. Henry smiled.

Immediately slowing down and turning off his headlights so he wouldn't alert them to his presence, Henry looked at the street and tried to imagine where they were going. No other businesses were open for them to slip into. No vehicles were parked on the street, so if they had one, it was likely in the lot behind the buildings. He pulled to the curb and waited to see what they would do. To see if the universe had provided.

The one with the long red hair, obviously a bottle tint even from this distance, lit a cigarette and leaned back against the brick of the building. The other didn't follow suit but seemed to be carrying the conversation as the smoker watched the brunette's face, nodding occasionally.

"Oh my God, they're going to just stand right there. Stand there and smoke." Henry's smile turned into a quiet giggle. He looked at the businesses and apartment windows above them again, and he found no signs of life. These two girls were the only people on this strip of sidewalk. Alone, waiting for him.

How long does it take to smoke a cigarette?

What do I do? Do I sneak up on them? How? On an empty street, I stand out like a sore thumb. Unless…

Henry shoved the small Mason jar in the oversized pocket of his fall jacket, tucked the ice pick into his back pocket, and stepped from the car. He shut the door as he normally would—not slamming it, but not quiet either. He didn't want to appear sneaky or alarm them. He watched the girls as he did, and was rewarded when the redhead glanced his way only long enough to spot the noise, before turning her attention back to her friend. *Or girlfriend?* Henry wondered what level their relationship was on as he strolled down the sidewalk.

His plan was simple. Act like he belonged there. Act like he was going to visit someone in one of the apartments. Act like he was so normal and boring they wouldn't have a reason to notice him. He pulled out his phone and pretended to text as he walked, gripping the phone with one hand and tapping random keys with his thumb. His other hand firmly gripped the ice pick still in his back pocket, squeezing and releasing in an anxious rhythm.

As he approached the girls, he nodded to himself as if he were reacting to something on his phone. He looked up at the apartment windows above them like he was searching, and slipped the phone back into his pocket. He glanced at the redhead and she gave him the standard thin, quick, insincere smile reserved for strangers in public. He mimicked it back to her. As he passed behind the girl who was talking, he smiled as he watched the redhead's smile turn to a look of horror.

Henry quickly wrapped his left hand around the brunette's head and forcefully grabbed her chin to hold her tight. His other hand brought the ice pick up to her neck and put the metal tip to her skin.

"Don't move or she dies." He ignored the whimper and gulping motion under his hand and watched the redhead's face absorb what was happening. She was rapt for a moment, the streetlight behind him catching the shine of fear in her eyes.

He knew the words were empty. They would *both* die. But he needed to control how. Where. And in what order.

The redhead dropped her cigarette. "Oh Kals. Oh God. I'm… I'm sorry." She turned and ran, leaving her friend in Henry's grip.

"Run, Alicia!" The brunette's cry escaped from between Henry's fingers, as her leg lifted and her foot slammed down into his own.

He watched the other girl run. He heard his captive spur her forward. She never looked back.

She just left her friend? Left her to die?

He couldn't fathom what either of them had been thinking. The whole plan had gone sideways so fast, and he suddenly had very little time to control the situation. For the briefest of moments, he considered letting her go and running the other direction. But the need for the blood overrode logic.

With panic turning to rage, he stabbed the brunette's neck repeatedly to kill her as quickly as possible, to stop her from shouting. The blood spurted each time he withdrew the ice pick, coating his hand and testing his grip on the weapon.

She wiggled, frantic, and flailed her arms. Adjusting his hold on her chin to keep her from escaping, he sidestepped and exposed his core, taking a solid fist to the groin as she continued to fight. He let out a howl and pulled her chin roughly, sharply, back toward him, stopping her free movement. The motion straightened her neck and let the blood run free. He felt her chest buck several times as she gasped and convulsed, before going limp in his arms.

He dropped to his knees with her body, not expecting

her dead weight to be so suddenly heavy. Henry took several deep breaths, as the sharp pain in his groin was accented by the throbbing in his foot where he'd stomped on him. He struggled to ignore his own pain and deal with the situation.

He looked at her eyes to check for life before releasing her neck. He set the ice pick down and reached into his pocket, pulling the jar free. Quickly uncapping it, he held it to her neck and gathered as much of the spilling blood as he could.

He looked down the street. The redhead was nowhere to be seen. He didn't know which way she'd gone—into an alley or side street, or into another apartment. He watched, fearful of her return, as his breathing climbed toward hyperventilating and his eyes burned with a budding stress headache. He looked back and saw the blood flow had slowed almost to a stop. He grabbed the lid, capped the jar, and stood, dropping her lifeless body to the sidewalk with a soft thud. Henry jogged back to his car and got inside, safe in its darkness. He watched the street for a moment before starting the car. He turned around and slowly drove back the way he'd come, forcing himself to stay under the speed limit.

Henry was not prepared for them to fight. He was not prepared for them to run. He was not prepared to take on two of them at once. The couple on the football field had made him feel invincible, given him unwarranted faith in his abilities. Yes, he had the blood of a female. But another had seen him, and gotten away.

TWENTY-EIGHT

Andrea ate dinner alone. A boring meal of reheated bits she hadn't really enjoyed the first time. But it was Monday, and Monday was leftover day—since anything remaining could be put out for the garbage on Tuesday. She'd picked at the remnants of a pork roast and discolored, overcooked potatoes.

She could feel the silent accusations of Dillon's empty place setting the entire time she ate, and glanced at the door occasionally. He hadn't answered her phone call. He hadn't responded to her texts. He hadn't contacted her at all.

In turn, she hadn't set him a place at the table. She hadn't prepared him a plate and left it covered in the microwave. Andrea had cooked, served, eaten and cleaned up afterward as if she lived alone.

Sitting in her chair watching the news, her panic grew. Every horrible lamian act they cited, or showed, or argued about, only convinced her further that her son was a full-blown murderer. It didn't scare her—it sickened her. Shamed her. She'd have to answer for it. She'd be held somehow responsible. She would be guilty of not stopping it when she could. And now he wasn't under her roof, under her care. He was loose on the world.

What *scared* her was he'd been missing for three days. She had no way of knowing when he would attack.

Will he just come strolling in to kill me? Or will he wait until I've gone to bed?

Andrea had debated changing the locks. She seriously

considered moving, or a hotel for a temporary solution. But after watching crime after crime on television, she knew if he wanted her dead, he'd get in, he'd find her. She needed *him* found. She needed him *home*.

She needed to take care of the situation, before it took care of *her*.

Andrea grabbed her phone and dialed the police.

"911—What's your emergency?"

The female voice answered so fast, it took Andrea off-guard and she almost screamed into the phone in surprise. "My son is missing."

"Okay ma'am, stay calm, I need to ask a couple questions. How old is your son?"

Andrea looked at the pictures on the wall. "He's seventeen"

"Oh. Okay. And when did you last see him?" The woman's tone changed from concern to pity.

"Friday morning, before school."

"Is there any reason to believe he is in danger? Does he take any medication or have any conditions?"

Andrea hadn't been prepared for the question, hadn't thought about people who deal with runaways or the real fears they experience when their own lives aren't in danger. "Um, no."

"Okay. Can you hold please?"

"I guess." Andrea heard Muzak before she'd answered the question and knew the operator had asked only as a polite gesture. Several moments of a song she knew but couldn't quite place, redone as an instrumental for use in elevators and on phone calls, stopped abruptly when a new voice questioned her. A male voice.

"Evening ma'am. I'm Officer Bollard. What's your name and your son's name?"

"I, um… Andrea. Andrea Hubbard. My son is Dillon

Hubbard."

"And you last saw him Friday?"

"Yes, sir. That's correct."

"Is it unusual for him to be gone from the home overnight?"

"Well, yeah." Andrea could hear the background sounded different than the silence of the 911 operator's room and wondered what department she had been transferred to.

"And did you check with his friends?"

"Uh, I don't *know* of any. He's not really close to anyone."

"Okay, ma'am. I understand. This can be difficult. But given his age and the time of year, it's highly possible he's just sowing his oats and exploring his boundaries."

"But it's been three days...I waited twenty-four hours." Andrea didn't understand why the officer didn't sound more concerned that a minor was missing.

"That's actually not a thing, ma'am. You can report someone missing after an hour. They use the twenty-four-hour or two-day rule on television for dramatic effect. If he's missing, he's missing, and you shouldn't have to wait before you worry."

Andrea almost said she wasn't worried because he was missing, but because he might come home unexpectedly. Instead, she muttered an incoherent acknowledgement.

"Now then, I'll get your address and have someone stop by to pick up a picture, and we'll keep a look out for him. Have you contacted the school, to see if he was in his classes?"

"No. I haven't. I mean... I figured he'd be home today and when he didn't... well I called you."

"Okay, no problem, ma'am. It's perfectly normal to worry and not think of even the simplest things. Have you been fighting lately?"

"Uh, no. No, he's not a mean kid." She answered without thinking and then paused on her reflexive reply.

He's not. Never has been.

But now… now he's got those teeth.

"And is he, or either you or your spouse, a lamian?"

"Why? Why is that a question?" She sat upright in her chair, defensive, ready to lie to protect herself.

"Well, I'm also going to ask his height and weight, and both birth and current gender. It's just among the questions so we have a full report, ma'am. No need to take offense."

"Oh, I wasn't *offended*, just…not sure why it mattered."

"Sadly, it matters if we have to identify a body. But let's not think about that, let's find your son and get him home."

"Oh…" Andrea didn't know how to respond to possibility they'd actually find him and bring him home.

There was a sudden rise in the noise behind the officer. Shouting and commotion of some sorts had turned whatever department she was talking to into chaos. The officer's tone changed. An urgency that had nothing to do with Andrea seemed to spurn him into wrapping up the conversation.

"Can I get your address so I can send a uniform over to get a picture and look around a bit?"

Andrea gave the officer her address and thanked him. She hung up the phone and sat back in the chair. She'd done what was expected and reported him missing.

Now if they found him, could she do what she *should?*

TWENTY-NINE

"I couldn't see his face. I couldn't see anything other than that shiny silver stick he had pushed up against her throat." The girl was visibly trembling.

"I'm sorry, Alicia. I know you've had a rough night and the morning hasn't been much better. But if you can tell me *anything* about the attacker—*anything at all*—maybe that will be the key to catching him." Detective Connor Murphy furrowed his brows at her obvious pain.

"I don't know what else I can tell you. He was taller than Kals, probably three inches, but she's—she *was*—sorta short, so that doesn't make him *too* tall, maybe five-eight. The streetlight was behind him, so his face was all dark." Her eyes flit across the floor as if the answer could be among the pattern there.

"Was he at all familiar to you? His voice maybe?" Connor had rolled his chair around to sit next to her, in a more casual manner, rather than trying to talk from across the desk in a cold, more formal fashion. He needed to know what she knew, what she saw. He needed her to trust him and feel safe. He sat close enough to be able to speak softly in the busy squad room.

"I… I don't know. I ran. I panicked and I ran. We had *literally* just watched the news about this guy and I wanted a cigarette. Kals wouldn't let me go outside by myself and was joking about how if he ever came for us, to remember he was only *one* person and we were *two,* and so whoever he didn't grab should run." She paused and looked up at Connor, leaning forward like she was telling him something important he didn't know. "I mean, he doesn't *hurt* people. He *kills* them. So if he's got you, you're done for, *right*? So I ran." Her face wrinkled up, as she burst into another fit of tears as her hands came up to hold the sides of her head and frame her face. "Oh my God, I ran away and left her to die!"

Connor held out a box of Kleenex, and let her cry for a couple minutes. There was no point pushing her if she wasn't ready. When she was ready, she took several tissues, wiped her face and blew her nose. A heavy sigh was her way of saying she was ready to continue.

He put the box down next to her and reached over to his desk. He grabbed the file, flipping through it for the pictures. *Shiny silver stick.* But Connor had another idea as well.

"You said you were watching the story about him?"

"Yeah…" Her red-rimmed eyes looked at him with concern.

"Did either of you recognize any of the names of the *other* victims?"

She shook her head. "No. Not that I remember. I mean, she didn't say anything, so I don't think so. She would have said *something* if she knew one of them." The girl looked at the file in his hand with concern. "Why? Did they know each other?"

"Not so far. No." He shrugged and pulled two small photos out of the file. Alicia pulled back with a look of horror and he realized she thought they were crime scene photos. "No no, hon. Nothing horrible. Just… here." He turned the pictures toward her. "Did his weapon look anything like either of these?"

The left photo was a picture of an orbitoclast, which he'd had to look up when the coroner first mentioned it. It was a surgical instrument, which had been designed and used for transorbital lobotomies before the procedure's popularity waned in the late 1950s. It was a solid piece of metal, thinner than a pencil and approximately ten inches long. It started as a sharp spike, and then tapered into a shaft ending with a handle shaped a bit like a pull-cord grip. They were no longer sold or used by the medical profession, but antique dealers and eBay had several on the market. And both Connor *and* the coroner, Rogers, thought it possible he was using this as some sort of twisted fantasy weapon.

The picture on the right showed a standard, run-of-the-mill ice pick available at any department store or hardware counter. A weapon of convenience Connor felt came without any connotations of fantasy or otherwise. The example in the photo was eight inches long—half the length was a wooden handle with the pick itself coming from the center of it.

She flinched. "That. I think." She pointed to the photo on the right. "He was holding it, so I couldn't really *see* the handle, but I could see the *end* of it. I could see it *had* a handle. A dark, dirty handle…" Her complexion washed out to a pale sickly tone.

Connor thought she might throw up right there on his shoes.

She gasped as she looked down. "Was that blood on the handle?"

"Oh miss, don't. Don't get upset like that. It was dark. It could have been dirt, or the design in the wood stain. You can't assume it was blood. That will just upset you. Please. Don't." He put a hand on her shoulder in an attempt to soothe her. "But you're sure there was a handle."

She nodded without looking up at him.

"Was there anything else, anything at all? His shoes?

Was he wearing a uniform? Anything."

She shook her head, but suddenly lifted it and looked Connor in the eye. "Wait. He had a phone. It was really small, I remember that. He was texting someone right before he attacked and I remember thinking his phone was really little, not like mine." She pulled out her phone and held it up for him to see. She had the newest iPhone model, which so many people complained was too big.

"Okay, okay. That's good." Connor wrote down the information on the inside of the file folder. He knew he couldn't track the man on that alone. It wasn't enough to even begin a search. But he could use it once they caught him—to tie him to *this* case. *This* witness. "Anything else?"

She shook her head. "No. I'm sorry." Her tears started again, as she grimaced and tried to keep her sobs to herself. "It just… it happened so fast. I wasn't paying attention to him. Just some random boring-looking guy walking, and then I was running."

"It's okay. You did really well. And if you remember anything, you can call us. I'll get an officer to take you home." He stood and cocked his head at some disturbance in the front lobby. He suddenly wondered if she'd prefer to avoid the apartment until the crew had cleaned up the sidewalk. "Or is there somewhere else you'd rather go?"

The return of gentle sobs and more tears had reduced her to head nods and he put a hand on her shoulder to acknowledge it. "Alright, hang on a minute. I'll be right back." He gently put the box of tissues in her lap before heading out to the lobby.

Connor walked out into the hallway with concern and curiosity mixed into his expression of annoyance. "What the—" He turned the corner by the holding cell and froze. "Oh shit."

A dozen or so citizens had taken it upon themselves to come into the lobby and harass the desk sergeant or anyone who would listen. Connor noticed they were all women, ranging from their late twenties to late forties, and then he recognized two of them.

Oh hell, the fucking PTA is here?

They spoke over each other in their agitated state and Connor could only catch snippets of their complaints.

"You're protecting the vampires."

"Why aren't you trying harder to catch this guy?"

"If he was killing vampires, there would be riots and you'd be forced to find him."

"You're feeding our children to them. To those monsters!"

Connor cocked his head at the last comment's owner. He couldn't remember her name, but knew she was the mother of one of Tamara's classmates—and not someone he ever would have pinned for being a bigot, with her big smile and overly gracious attitude at every bake sale and student event.

"We're not food. Our babies are not food. Why aren't you out there trying to stop this?"

Wow. Three times we've told the public it's not a lamian, but they continue to believe what they want. He gave the desk sergeant a look of pity. The man threw back a desperate expression, a plea for help, but Connor wasn't about to engage with this group.

Connor shook his head and looked around the lobby, settling on two large uniformed officers. "For fuck's sake, guys. I've got a witness back here who is already in tears and you've let *this* in the front door? Get these people out of here."

THIRTY

Madison had been picking at her bandaged fingertips all day, but not because she was nervous about her teeth anymore—not since Tamara's visit on Monday. The two of them had gone to the meeting at the Lamplight Foundation, and Madison had been blown away by the eclectic group and had barely scratched the surface of knowledge lining the walls inside. Afterward, they'd stopped at Dairy Queen for a Blizzard and a pep talk about bravery.

Tamara reminded her of all the times Madison's parents had expressed tolerance and fought for the rights of the lamians. She asked about her dad's side having the gene with, "Isn't there an aunt or someone? No one seemed upset by it." She was right. Madison's parents *knew* it was in the bloodline. Tamara convinced her they wouldn't, couldn't, react the way Madison feared. By the time the girls drank the last bit of their melted Blizzards, Madison was ready to walk in the door and tell her parents.

Her mother had been so relieved to find out Madison wasn't going through some anorexic fad, she'd started crying and immediately suggested ice cream to celebrate. Madison laughed and told her she and Tamara had already splurged. Her parents raised their eyebrows at Tamara's name and nodded in approval, her father declaring, "Good, we missed that girl."

The rest of the evening had been Madison bonding with parents she had somehow believed would disown her. She hadn't realized how pulled back from them and distant she'd become in the last few weeks until she found out her dad had gotten a raise they'd celebrated, with her at the table in the restaurant with them, and she hadn't even registered why they were there. But her secret was out and she was back, part of the family again. A family she had always known to be very loving, if not slightly shy—which always made her wonder where she got the outgoing gene from.

Probably the same relative who gave me the teeth.

Her parents were delighted to hear about the group meetings on Mondays and offered to go with her, suggesting they sit with Tamara's mom separately if the girls wanted to be away from their parents. They discussed the doctor appointments that would need to happen, and shared stories of people they knew who had gone through this and what they thought they could expect.

Madison's mother excitedly started looking for lamian-based cooking shows. "I was getting really bored with spaghetti and chicken anyway." And in the end, Madison went to bed feeling better about everything. Her life was back to the way it had been.

Except for Brenna.

Brenna would never accept this. But throughout the day, as she picked at her bandages, Madison had come to the conclusion she'd be better off without Brenna. She had always been closer to Tamara, and other than Amber, Brenna also had Tristan—the two of them needed no one else in their lives. She didn't know how to disclose the secret to the judgmental girl with a bigger social media following than the local celebrities on the news.

Madison told Tamara she planned to whisper it to Brenna during Chemistry, since it was the only class they had together and Madison could easily avoid Brenna for the rest of the day afterward. Madison thought it would be quieter to do it during a class where there was a teacher and a room full of students, and Brenna would be less likely to cause a scene, if only for her *own* self-preservation.

But Madison had chickened out.

After Chemistry class, Tamara was waiting by Madison's locker believing the deed done. A confused Amber stood next to her, looking between the outcast and the two coming down the hall. The panic washing across Madison's face did not go unnoticed by Brenna, as they walked together toward the locker.

"What's this? Flirting with the enemy?" Brenna sped up, getting to the locker before Madison and flopping her back against the metal door with a loud ding. "What's up, *Fanger*? Think you're going to wiggle your way back in?"

Tamara looked from Brenna to Madison, and Madison shrugged apologetically.

"You know no one wants you around, right? Not now. Not now that we know *what* you are, why would we bother? Not a human, not an animal. What are you?"

Tamara said nothing and let Brenna dribble her hate speech. Several other students stopped in the hallway to whisper and point at the drama.

"You probably know the fanger killing people, don't you? My mom says the cops will never catch him because they're protecting him. Protecting all of you because you're fucking minorities and if they don't then you'll riot like they did down in New Orleans." Brenna cocked her head for a minute. "Oh hey, the cops… and here's the cop kid… I suppose your father's leading the rally to let this bullshit happen." Brenna reached forward to poke at Tamara, but Tamara blocked her and swatted Brenna's hand out of the way.

"Who in your life hates you so much that you have

to act like this to others?" Tamara's voice was so obviously condescending, Madison thought she'd burst out laughing, but she feared Brenna would snap and the girl's temper would rear its ugly head.

"What did you say?" Brenna narrowed her eyes at Tamara.

"You. All this hate you have for everyone who's not exactly like you, or at least trying to *be* you, or *worship* you. Where's that coming from? Mommy doesn't show you enough attention?"

Brenna's eyebrows went up and Madison braced for violence. Madison hadn't actually seen Brenna do anything in years, but one third-grade recess ended with *two* boys crying and Brenna *laughing* through her own bloody nose. It left enough of a memory to be wary.

Instead, Brenna spun at Madison—her bobbing curls framed her wide brown eyes shadowed with purple liner and a sudden core of indignation. "You're just going to stand there and let her talk to me like that, Maddie?"

Madison backed up a step, out of reach, and nodded her head. "Yeah. Yeah, I am." Madison lifted her lip and showed the new tooth growing into the empty socket, knowing she wouldn't need to say anything after showing Brenna the reality.

"Oh for fuck's sake. Really? So you're one of them, too. Well good fucking riddance then. The two of you can skip off together and have a happy life. I sure as shit don't want anything to do with you. Dirty vampires. *Animals.* Your kind should never have come out of hiding."

Tamara shook her head and stepped closer to Madison, nudging her and indicating she look behind Brenna.

"You're a real piece of work, you know that, Brenna?" Tristan stepped closer and looked down at his girlfriend, the basketball player's face showing as much disgust as his voice indicated. "These are your *oldest* friends."

"Not anymore." Brenna held a hand up as if to shoo them away, and then wrapped her arm around his and smiled brightly at Amber.

Tristan pulled free from her grasp. "Yeah, I think maybe we're done. For good, this time."

"What? You can't be serious." Brenna looked up at him with genuine shock.

"What if I have the gene? What if my teeth fall out?"

"But you don't. They won't. You're human. You're perfectly human." Brenna grabbed his hands and tried to pull them to her chest.

Again, he wiggled free.

"Yeah, I am. But you're a bitch, Brenna, and I don't need that in my life. I've got scholarships and college offers, and I don't need to drag you and your hate with me when I get out of here." Tristan turned and walked away, pushing through a small group of students who had gathered to watch. The crowd immediately began whispering as he moved beyond them.

"Tristan!" Brenna called after him but he never slowed, never turned back.

Amber's eyes widened and she looked at the three of them. Without a word she backed up two steps and became part of the crowd of onlookers. She'd never been outspoken, she'd never been brave. Madison saw her actions and knew neither of those traits would change today.

Across the hallway, leaning against a locker, a boy in a plain white tee and a pair of purposely-distressed jeans had watched the whole thing. "It's okay, Brenna. I hate them all too."

"Fuck off, Blake." Brenna spat at him and huffed. She stormed off, away from the sounds of Tamara and Madison snickering.

THIRTY-ONE

Henry screwed the lid onto the Mason jar and put it back in the fridge. There was enough left in the bottom to fill a Dixie cup. He needed to be frugal and hoard what little bit he had. He returned to his well-worn couch and sat down in front of the ten o'clock news.

But it's so good. He thought of the jar in the refrigerator.

It was hard for Henry to control himself. He'd gone into the jar three times since dinner. Each time, he'd only allowed himself to lick off whatever coagulated chunks would stick to the butter knife he swirled through the depleting supply.

I knew she'd taste better. I knew it was because she was a female.

The half a jar worth he'd managed to salvage from the girl on the street wasn't going to make it to midnight with his current state of need versus restraint. He needed more than a single jar. He *wanted* it more often now, and in larger quantities.

And not always to eat. Henry smiled and put a hand on his upper thigh, applying pressure as he slid his fingers down, wrapped them around the underside of his leg, and pulled his hand back up firmly, as if teasing himself with the idea, seducing his own mind with possibilities. He shook the idea loose. There wasn't enough blood to make it worth it. Henry needed to go hunting.

Maybe I should still get a lamian. Just to see. What if female lamian is even better than just female?

Henry sat a little taller.

What if male *lamian was even better?*

His desire to become one of them had twisted into something new. He no longer cared if *they* accepted him. He had the teeth. He was as close as he could get to being one of them and they couldn't take it away from him. He could *identify* as a lamian in today's social climate and they'd have to accept him as such.

At face value anyway. Not on his medical records. Not yet.

There was no news about his murders tonight. Or at least nothing new had developed for them to share, which was good. It meant they weren't any closer to catching him. But they were most likely looking harder than they had. He'd have to be more careful. Especially since the redhead from Monday had escaped. He knew they had talked to her. They must have by now. It's been days. And she had seen him. Looked right at him and smiled. She could describe him.

But she doesn't know me. Can't name me.

It's been four days and no one has come knocking.

He felt safe enough, for the moment, and his mind wandered back to the blood he could still taste. He needed to hunt, but he needed to lay low.

Maybe go over to Springfield, or down by the docks where the vagrants sleep. I wonder what they taste like.

He pictured their filthy skin, and the dirt and grime and germs that would flow into the blood if he were to choose one of the water bums. He shuddered in disgust and swallowed down the idea of bile. No matter how desperate he became, he couldn't stoop low enough to bother with the homeless.

His tongue flicked across the teeth he'd glued in against doctor's orders. They felt strong, sturdy, and worked fine when he ate and held up when he brushed them. Now it was about the blood he could imagine they'd harvest. The blood he could swirl and swish in his mouth. The blood he didn't need on a genetic level, but on a mental level had become highly addicted to.

And he was almost out. Again.

Living jar to jar is worse than paycheck to paycheck.

Henry remembered when he'd had several jars at once, only a couple weeks ago, when he wasn't gorging himself on the precious liquid. He needed to find restraint again. He needed to keep stock.

I need a steady supply.

The idea struck him without warning and the meaning of it took a moment to sink in. Henry watched the weatherman on television talk but wasn't listening. He was rolling an idea around, poking at it ever so gently to see if it was viable.

A supply, rather than a victim.

On tap, as needed.

Henry's mouth became wet with the saliva of excitement.

If there's no body to find, they'll think I've stopped.

Stop killing. Keep drinking.

Henry's lips spread into a wide smile.

Not a victim, but a captive.

How? Where?

He looked at the basement door. It was only a partially finished basement, but it was dry and had no exterior entrance of its own, no windows to break in. Or out.

He could easily build a small room. *A cage with solid walls.*

Add some soundproofing, a better lock at the top of the stairs, and it would take minimal effort, and almost no money, to create the perfect holding pen. A *flesh* refrigerator to keep his blood supply warm, and steady.

Excitement built like a blush in his face, warming his skin and widening his grin. His eyes almost watered with adrenaline, at the thought of what he would have.

Yes. A captive.

Henry turned the television off and headed for the basement. He'd need to measure the area, make a list, and plan how he'd spend his weekend. He could survive a couple days without a new jar. Especially knowing what was waiting on the other side.

THIRTY-TWO

Dillon stared into the open fridge, taking inventory of the choices offered by the Lamplight Foundation. He was surprised by how much fruit and vegetables they ate, even though they didn't have to.

Victoria had explained, "If for nothing else, the flavor and texture is a nice change. Plus, unless you're raised by lamians in a strict dietary household, you spend the first two decades of your life eating all those things. You develop favorites."

He had understood the logic, but it didn't help any of it look any more appealing to Dillon before eight in the morning. He'd never really been a breakfast kid.

He grabbed a single-serving orange juice bottle he could drink on the way, and he shut the fridge, turning around to see Max standing in the doorway.

God, that guy can sneak up on a person.

"Can we talk?" Maximilian was almost two hundred years old, and in truth didn't look a day over eighty-five. But it wasn't his looks commanding Dillon's attention. It was the tone of his voice.

Dillon glanced at the clock on the wall. "Uh, sure. I've got time."

"I can drive you if you want. We can talk on the way."

"Nah, it's all good. I like walking." Dillon pulled one of the wooden chairs away from the kitchen table and sat down. "What's up?"

Max followed suit but seemed immediately uncomfortable in the chair. The rounded modern design was obviously not his choosing, and Dillon realized he'd only ever seen the man relax in the wooden high-back chairs of the library rooms. Max laced his fingers together and set them on the table. "The school called."

"Oh?" Dillon furrowed his brows in thought. "I haven't done anything."

"No no. You haven't. Seems your mother has filed a missing person's report though. The police then do a follow-up with the school. You haven't been marked absent so they don't consider you a runner—only what the principal referred to as a *hider*." Max shrugged. "Which, I guess, is exactly what you are."

"Okay. Is that a problem? I thought you said I could stay here. That you'd help me emancipate."

"Yes, and I will, but they called looking for you."

Dillon's eyes widened. He didn't want to deal with his mother. He didn't want her knowing where he was. "You didn't—"

"No, I didn't. I feel she is a threat to your safety. And while I won't tell the school that, if a police officer or a judge asked me, I would tell them exactly what I think of the situation."

"So you believe me?"

Max sighed, and Dillon was surprised to see him relax his shoulders in a pseudo-slump for half a beat before sitting upright again. "Truth be told, I may have gone past your house on one of my nightly walks. And yes, I may have eavesdropped."

Dillon raised his eyebrows in mock surprise. Max was always about the rules being established for a reason. His behavior was never anything other than stellar, proper. And here he was admitting he had spied on the thoughts of someone in their own home.

"I still think it's rude, but I needed to know the extent

of your concerns."

"You mean you needed to know if I was lying."

Max inhaled slowly, deliberately taking his time and choosing his words.

"Yes." He exhaled through his nose like a tired dragon. "You are new, and therefore your thoughts are a jumble, and not all of them can be easily read. And to invite you into my home with the threat of danger to follow? Yes, I needed to know if you were lying."

"And? I'm not, am I?"

"Well, while I didn't hear a direct threat toward you, I heard enough anger and hatred to know she's not likely to come around anytime soon and it's probably best for you to stay here. To stay out of her way."

Dillon sat back in his chair and put his arms behind his head. It was a cocky gesture meant to declare himself the victor. The feeling of satisfaction was fleeting.

"You need to call her though. And tell the school. I won't disclose information to the school without your consent, and I didn't have it yet. You simply need to stop at the principal's office and let them know you are staying with me. We've done this before and they know you are safe here." Max paused for a breath. "And seriously, call her and tell her you're safe. You don't have to tell her *where*, maybe say you're at a shelter."

"Okay. I can do that." Dillon pushed out the chair to stand and Max shook his head.

"One more thing. We need to talk about these murders."

"We? *Why*?" Dillon was instantly confused and defensive.

"I need to know where you've been at night lately."

"You've *got* to be kidding me!" Dillon's voice echoed lightly in the large room. "You think I'm the monster she expects me to be?"

"I didn't say that, Dillon. I said, *we need to talk about it*." Max stared at him, his age showing on his face.

"Oh… you mean you want to talk about it, *and* listen to my thoughts about it."

Max nodded. "Yes, but not for the reasons you may think. You may have seen something, may know something, and not realize it."

"Whatever man. Do what you gotta do."

"I know you leave the house at night. Where do you go?"

"The park. I wander my way through it and head back. Just fresh air, clear my head, no big thing."

"Is that where you go on Mondays when we have group?"

"Yeah. I don't do people, especially groups. I've got you and Vic and the library. I don't need to sit with a bunch of people and ask questions."

"Understandable. And after school? You always walk straight back here?"

"Usually, unless I'm at the Quikmart." He flicked a thumb at the schedule stuck to the refrigerator with a magnet from an out-of-business pizza place. "On those days, I'm down there with old man Mundy until eight or so. And then I walk back here." Dillon glanced at the clock. "If this is gonna go for a bit, maybe you should give me a ride."

"Let me grab my keys." Max stood without further provocation, and Dillon wondered what he could possibly think Dillon knew.

THIRTY-THREE

"Ohhh, how I missed your mom's sandwiches." Tamara almost groaned the comment, her delight obvious, and took another bite of the ham and cheese she'd traded her hot lunch ticket for.

"Yeah, you're nuts." Madison shook her head at her friend and stabbed the plastic fork into the pile of lettuce and tomato on her plate. "I'll take the pizza and salad bar over *that* any day."

"Hey, good job, you two." An underclassman in khakis and a flannel paused long enough at the table to compliment them and walk away. The girls looked at each other, the unspoken question of *who* lingered on both of their faces. They shrugged, snickering with their mouths full. It hadn't been the *first* well-wisher of the day.

Word of their altercation with Brenna had spread through the school like wildfire. Most likely having made its way from the prom queen to the last loner of ninth grade by the time they'd gotten home last night, but they weren't aware of it.

Until they got to school Friday morning.

Hopping out of the police cruiser—Tamara's dad dropping them both off and declaring there would be *no more walking* for either of them—they were met by a small group of well-known lamians, who proceeded to slow clap as they walked past. Madison and Tamara looked at each other in confusion, but by the time they hit their lockers they realized what had happened.

Word had spread. And Brenna wasn't too happy

about it from the unwanted, unrequested reports they each received throughout the morning.

Depending on who was passing along the information, it may have been one of the girls who told Brenna off, or it may have been Tristan. Either way, the end of the story was the same—Brenna missed her last few classes yesterday and was seen in full-on tears climbing into her mother's SUV. And she wasn't in school today.

"So…" A hot lunch tray slid down the table to land next to Madison. Dillon settled onto the bench in front of it. "I hear you two had an exciting day yesterday. Took ya long enough."

"Took us—" Tamara laughed and shook her head. "Grudge alive and well still?"

"What? Kindergarten? I don't care. But seriously though, good riddance." He lifted the school's idea of a special treat toward his mouth—the under-seasoned, overly greasy, cheese pizza available only on Fridays—and spoke with a grin before biting into it. "You've both been better than that glue-sniffer since you learned to tie your shoes."

"So… are you one?" Madison didn't care to talk about Brenna. It hurt. It was still horrible to lose a friend, even if it was for the best. And she didn't want to linger on it. She wanted to move forward, starting now.

Dillon nodded the entire time he chewed and swallowed. "Yup. As of a week into summer vacation last year."

"Mine fell out in August," Tamara proffered and then cocked her head at Dillon. "Wait, what are we now? What is this? Some sort of club?"

Dillon almost choked on his next bite and had to take a drink from his chocolate milk carton to get it down. "Hell no. Just a nod and a hello, and then we'll go back to pretending we don't know each other."

"You don't have to do that." Madison's expression twisted up into an almost pout. "We've known each other forever. No reason we can't be friends."

Dillon tried to cover up his reaction, but Tamara saw it and smiled directly at him. He looked between the girls. "I don't know… what *tricks* have you two learned? Can I trust you?"

"Tricks?" Madison looked confused. "Ohhhh, oh that. I *think* I had a vision."

"Really?" Dillon leaned closer, his honest intrigue obvious.

"Yeah. I saw those two kids before they were killed, but when I saw them, it looked like they were all bloody."

"Seriously? That's *nasty*, Maddie. Why didn't you tell me?" Tamara's mouth hung open and her eyes squinted in disgust.

"It's been kind of crazy. Forgot I guess. Do *you* see things?" Madison asked the open air between them and looked at each in turn.

"Oh I wouldn't *want* that. No. But I get the serious heebie-jeebies sometimes. Maybe I'm going to have that sixth sense thing, what'd they call it?"

"Clairsentience, or sent-i-*ent*? One of those." Madison shrugged and took another bite of her salad, trying not to look overly curious about what ability Dillon might have.

"They? Who they?" Dillon finished his milk and opened a second carton. Madison noticed he did not tell them what, or if, he could do anything psychic.

"The Lamplight Foundation. It's a lamian group over by the park." Tamara answered excitedly. "They're in the old bed-and-breakfast place, you know, the one everyone thought was haunted when we were little. They have a group meeting on Mondays to help newbies like us figure everything out and learn the history and such. You should come with us."

"That's actually not a bad idea."

The three of them looked up to see Mrs. Fidler had stopped behind Dillon and Madison, leaning down slightly to interject into the overheard suggestion.

"Nah, I'm all good." Dillon shook his head and put his hands up in front of him to decline the idea. "I'm staying there, so I get access whenever I want and don't have to deal with any group of anxious teens."

"Staying there?" Madison looked genuinely concerned. "What do you mean?"

"Ugh, my psycho bi—" He looked up at Mrs. Fidler and changed his wording. "—*beast* of a mother. I can't live with her anymore. It's not healthy. So I'm staying in one of their boarding rooms for now."

"That's awesome. That place is *so* cool." Madison's eyes lit up in a friendly but jealous expression.

"Maximilian is a class act. He'll take good care of you." Mrs. Fidler nodded her approval.

"You know Max?" Dillon looked up at her, squinting.

"Oh yeah. We go way back." Her smile widened, and Madison found herself looking at the teacher's teeth and wondering.

Tamara wasn't one to silently question anything and leaned forward as she point-blank asked, "Are you a lamian? How *old* are you?"

"It's not polite to ask a woman her age." Mrs. Fidler raised an eyebrow at her.

"Okay… how long have you been *teaching*?" Madison looked up at her, prepared to do the math.

"Since women earned the right to vote." She looked

at each of them. "Yes, let that sink in. I've been doing this class a long time. The social report that's due? It used to be about *gender*, not genes."

"Oh wow. I mean. Wow." Madison couldn't find words to express her awe.

Tamara's mouth opened but only to form a surprised but silent circle.

Dillon blinked away a shocked expression. "You look, um…"

"Really good for my age?" She chuckled at the obvious comment. "I know. You will, too."

Mrs. Fidler stood upright and turned to walk away, revealing Amber standing behind her.

"Is there room at the table for a human?" Amber's face was one of regret and sadness.

"Of course!" Madison grinned and pointed to the bench next to Tamara, noticing Tristan at the other end of the room watching them. As their eyes met, he nodded respectfully, as if to apologize from a distance, and walked his tray to the table of jocks.

THIRTY-FOUR

Henry had been in the basement the better part of the day. He'd gotten everything he needed after work on Friday and waited until after dinner to haul it into the house under the cover of darkness. He'd been cleaning and building since early that Saturday morning. He had paused long enough to get more coffee, later switching the caffeine for bottled water, and then a quick trip to the store for a replacement battery for his drill—so he could use it for the screws rather than manually twisting each one in with a screwdriver.

Surprisingly, the basement hadn't been too terribly dirty—even though it was mostly unused, except for holiday boxes and the portions of his mother's belongings he couldn't stomach getting rid of yet. There had been the *expected* dust and cobwebs up in the open boards of the thick beams of the floor joists. And the gray Berber carpet had needed odor-absorbing sprinkles and a good vacuuming—*twice*—to get rid of the smell of the old, forgotten space.

Surveying the area under the house, Henry had decided on the far corner. It would only need two walls, had a sewer pipe to attach a chain to, and a drain for dumping a waste bucket. It was the perfect place to create a small room with a heavy door for his would-be guest.

Guest.

He'd stopped referring to his eventual blood bank as a *captive* sometime during work on Friday afternoon. It felt mean, and Henry thought he was being nice by keeping them alive. Not mean at all, but rather, generous. And so, in his mind, it would be a *guest* he'd give a room with a bed and food, just as you would a visitor.

He built a simple structure, using two-by-fours for the bottom plate and vertical studs that reached to the heavy beams above for strength and security. Framing a doorway into the side that faced the stairs, he moved inside and began screwing plywood to the studs to make the walls.

He had originally considered soundproofing, but the materials—both acoustic tiles and the sound dampening insulation he'd found locally—cost more than he was prepared to spend. Paycheck to paycheck, with no credit cards or other means of spending outside his budget, meant he needed to get the essential supplies only. He'd decided he would have to keep a gag on his guest until they learned the rules. And although he thought the basement, lacking windows or an exterior door, would help keep the sound in, he *did* plan on a second layer of plywood—just to be safe. It was a cheap alternative, and something he could easily add on to the room on his *next* payday.

His thoughts drifted as he hung the boards to enclose the space. It started to feel like a room, the bare bulb he had hung up high in the floor joists began casting shadows on new walls, and his thoughts drifted toward the finished product. He would only need a few things to call the room ready, once the walls were up and the door was affixed.

He looked up as if he could see through the floor and thought of the layout of the house. The room sat right beneath the kitchen. Whenever he was feasting on blood, banging pots and pans to cook, or clinking the glasses in the cupboard in preparation for a drink, his guest might be able to hear. Might know what those noises meant.

Above the kitchen was his mother's room. He missed her, but he smiled at the fortunate turn of events in her absence. Her room had been mostly packed up—her belongings given away, sold, or stashed in the basement. Only her bed and dresser were still upstairs, and the broken music box she loved so much still sitting on the dresser because he didn't know exactly what to do with it. The mattress—no frame, no box spring—could be dragged down here for his guest.

No chairs or dressers though. Nothing she can stand on. She.

Henry smiled.

He knew he'd be choosing a female for his guest. He didn't know who, or from where. He would look over his various Facebook groups after dinner and see if anyone looked like the perfect target—single, not many friends, very few pictures with other people, quiet online so an absence won't be noticed for a while, if ever. Yes, Henry had an idea what criteria would make the perfect resident for his new little room without a view. On the physical side of things, he didn't really care if she was blonde or brunette, fat or thin, but thought a chubbier person might be easier to overpower *and* would have more body, more tissue, more blood. Or perhaps, if he could find someone who looked like his father's new wife. *Wouldn't that be—*

Henry shrieked in pain.

The idea of secret justice against his father had caused him to slip with the drill, and he'd dragged the bit through the edge of his finger below the first knuckle. The open pocket of flesh immediately burned from exposure to air and began to bleed heavily. Without thought, Henry shoved the wound to his mouth like a small child.

As his finger began to throb, Henry swallowed a spoonful of his own blood and pulled his hand away. He studied the wound, a gaping tear in his flesh with exposed meat beneath, and considered the taste in his mouth.

My own blood.

The thought had never occurred to him. It seemed wrong and twisted. He obviously couldn't survive for long if he fed on himself.

But what if... just a little?

He put the finger back to his mouth and let his tongue explore the injury, keeping the tissue wet, preventing it from clotting or resealing like a smaller wound will often do. He suckled at his finger, letting the taste wash over him mentally as the blood spread thin across his tongue.

How much can you swallow of your own blood before you pass out from blood loss?

He knew how much blood he could put in his stomach before he *vomited.* He'd learned that the very first time, with the jogger on the bridge. Too much, too fast, and his stomach reacted in panic as if it were his own internal injury. The nausea had taken him over less than a block away from the bridge and he'd had to pull over and vomit. All the beautiful blood he'd managed to suckle from the dead man's neck, wasted, laying there in the moonlight mixed with spit and bile on the loose gravel of the road's shoulder.

The second victim had gone much smoother. Henry had driven out to the bridge and sat in the dark with his headlights off, hoping for another jogger. Another *accident.* When nothing happened, he drove around the seedier parts of town. He couldn't stomach the idea of a homeless person, so he crossed the tracks and slowly drove through several of Riverside's unkempt trailer parks. The large man sleeping in his living room with his door wide open had been a fluke. *A present from the universe.* And he'd taken advantage of the gift.

Parking down the road, he backtracked through the dark lots to the trailer, slipped inside and shut the door. Sneaking quietly through the living room, he stopped in front of the heavy man and pulled the ice pick from his back pocket.

He'd purchased the ice pick at the hardware store over in Springfield the day before, knowing he wanted more blood, needed more, and what he'd have to do to get it. Some searching online taught him why the first one had bled the way he did, and Henry knew now he had to puncture deep enough to hit the interior jugular, the thicker of the two, which would flow better, longer, before collapsing. The key had worked enough because it had been a larger wound, and messy. This would be cleaner. Like the movies. Like the myth. A twisted metaphor, as a shiny silver *tooth* puncturing their veins for his meal.

The idea he was going to kill someone had never bothered him. He had only mildly, and quite briefly, wondered how long he'd been willing and not known it.

He looked at the unconscious man's neck and swung the ice pick a couple times to practice. As if it were nothing more than a golf swing you wanted to get right. Henry froze midair.

What if I miss?

Instead of swinging with a hopeful stab or possible frantic bevy of jabs, Henry had an idea. He held the ice pick still, barely off the man's neck and lined up where he wanted to strike. He watched the man's sleeping face, his steady breath, and smiled at the prospect of his short future. When Henry was sure of his placement, he brought his other hand down hard and fast and drove the pick into the man's neck.

The man immediately opened his eyes and tried to scream, but it came out a garbled tumble of unintelligible sounds as he immediately gurgled on his own blood. Henry put a knee to the man's groin and a hand to his shoulder, pinning him down. The pick had gone in much deeper than the key had with the jogger. The ice pick had pierced the skin and then sunk all the way to the handle, burying the steel beyond the intended vein and deep into the man's throat. He pulled the pick free and dropped it to the floor, retrieving the old pickle jar he'd brought with and putting it to the man's neck to collect the oozing blood.

Fascinated, he watched the man's expression as he gulped for air but only found blood. Henry didn't understand what was happening. He thought a stab to the neck would immediately kill the man like they showed in so many movies. He watched the man choke and gasp, coughing bloody spittle at Henry, as the man's eyes widened in fear before finally relaxing in death. Henry would learn later—as he searched the Internet for answers—the man's trachea had been stabbed as well. The man hadn't simply bled *out*, but he'd also bled internally. He had been initially unable to breathe, and then literally drowned in his own blood as the wound seeped into his lungs, while Henry was collecting it in the pickle jar.

When the man's heart stopped, the flow of blood turned to a trickle. Henry took the jar away and leaned in to suckle the blood around the wound, but pulled back at the last minute. He wasn't disposing of this body. He couldn't leave his saliva here.

And I have what I want.

Henry smiled at the blood. He capped the jar, retrieved the ice pick and slipped back outside—leaving the door open, exactly as he'd found it.

In the car, Henry had taken several gulps of the blood but felt his stomach almost immediately react like it had the previous time. He felt the nausea and a muscle spasm, which could precursor vomit, and stopped drinking. He capped the jar and realized he'd have to enjoy it in small doses. Or perhaps cook with it.

And it will last so much longer.

At least it used to last longer, Henry thought, as he pulled his damaged finger away from his mouth again. He looked from the wound to the half-built room.

His stomach grumbled and he panicked for a moment, before he realized he was hungry and not reacting to his own blood. He set the drill's battery in its charger and headed for the stairs. He'd done enough work for the day. He was eager for more blood, but knew he'd have it soon enough.

In the meantime, he had a fresh cow liver from the butcher sitting in a container in his fridge. He didn't care about the liver, so much as the blood it was swimming in. He could enjoy it after a quick meal of reheated leftover pizza. He knew it wouldn't be the same. He knew the liver and the blood wouldn't taste right. But he hadn't bought it to eat. He had purchased it for lubrication.

THIRTY-FIVE

Andrea braced the front door with a foot on either side of it, holding it still in its open state. The screen was closed and she reached over to flick the simple lock under the handle with her thumb for precautionary measures—as if someone who truly wanted to get inside couldn't rip the mesh panel. She glanced at the little bit of neighborhood she could see from her doorway. It was quiet. An unusually warm day for October, she would have expected more people out and about after church.

Maybe they're not home yet, or in their backyards. She pondered and listened beyond her living room television to the silence of neighbors among the tiny noises of nature outside. She could neither hear nor see *anyone.*

And hopefully, no one is paying attention to me either.

She grabbed the screwdriver from the top of the small bookcase near the front door and began taking the doorknob off. Changing the locks was as simple as swapping out the knobs on the front and back doors, as well as replacing the deadbolt. They were each the exact model as what was currently on the doors, but they came with new keys.

She needed to feel safer.

She was halfway there—glancing through the kitchen to the back door she'd just finished updating.

The brass knob came loose in her hand as soon as the first screw was pulled free, and she worried it wasn't enough to stop anyone anyway. But looking at the deadbolt above the knob, she reminded herself she had an enhanced level of protection.

She wasn't worried about Dillon being upset about his key not fitting. He'd suggested she do it, when he called to tell her he wasn't coming home.

When the phone rang the night before, Andrea had jumped, startled by the sudden noise in the otherwise quiet house.

She had turned the television off and was sitting in the living room, curled up on the couch with a baseball bat she'd found in the garage—buried in a large box of Dillon's forgotten sporting attempts. She wouldn't be able to hear him break in if the television was on, so she sat in silence, vigilant. But she was not prepared for the shrill barking of her cellphone's default ringer.

She grabbed at the phone to shut it up, but when she saw the name at the top of the screen, she froze rather than saying hello.

"Mom? Mom, are you there?"

Andrea could hear her son's voice and knew the silence would be mistaken for a bad connection and he'd just call back if she didn't answer.

"I'm here. Where are you?" She tried to sound like a worried parent, rather than a worried human. She tried to wrap her fear around the model of motherhood she was supposed to be.

"I'm safe. That's why I'm calling."

"Oh? But where? *Where* are you?" She glanced at the windows. "Why'd you leave?"

The silence on the phone made Andrea wonder why he was thinking so long about his answer. Was he going to lie? Was he outside?

"I don't feel safe there." Dillon's voice was soft, quiet, as if he'd whispered a secret to her.

"*You* don't feel—" She stopped herself from finishing,

hearing the inflection in her voice, the shock she felt at his words. *He doesn't feel safe? What about me?*

"I just think maybe it's for the best."

"For… Well, for how long?" She needed to be prepared for his return.

"Indefinitely, Mom. Unless you stop watching all that hate on television. I am what I am, Mom. And you hate what I am."

She couldn't argue with him. He was right and Andrea knew it. But she had no idea what to do or say now that he'd thrown it in her face.

"Have you ever even met another lamian, Mom? Have you ever had your *own* experience with one? Or just the crap you watch on TV?"

"I—" She tried to explain herself, suddenly on the defensive. *As if I'm the bad person here?*

"You're full of hate and fear, Mom. And you don't have a reason for either of them." She heard Dillon take a deep breath. "I'm at a safe house. And I'm staying here until I graduate. Then I'll get my own place and move out and figure out my life. If you want to be part of it, you can call me or text me. Maybe we can visit."

"You're going to leave me alone?" She meant it in the sense that he wasn't going to hurt her, but it sounded more like she was afraid to be abandoned.

"Yeah I am. Change the locks if it makes you feel better."

Oh God, he heard it the way I meant it.

"But your stuff—"

"I took what I wanted. If I need anything else, I can call you and set up a time to come get it."

"Are you sure?"

"I'm sure. Just know I'm fine." He paused a beat and added, "And so are you. Good-bye, Mom."

The phone went silent and she looked at it. The call timer had stopped. He'd hung up.

And her heart suddenly ached. The pictures on the wall didn't show a lamian—they showed her son. A son she had pushed away. A son she was still afraid of, a son she considered dead, but loved. Her internal conflict twisted into tears. Not a chest-heaving sob, but a quiet acceptance of loss. Silent tears ran down her face unchecked, and she eventually fell asleep, still clutching the baseball bat.

When she woke she knew she'd do exactly what he suggested and change the locks. Maybe he wouldn't come in and attack her, but it didn't hurt to be safe.

She went to church and the café as if nothing was wrong, never mentioning to the girls her son had run away. "*Moved out*," *sounds better*, she thought. She stopped and purchased the three replacement locks on her way home and was almost done adding a layer to her sense of security.

The television returned from commercial and the afternoon desk jockey for the weekend news program declared they had breaking video in the nationally covered altercation, which had happened the previous evening. Andrea tore the wrapper off and pulled the shiny brass knob free, her attention on the news program.

In a town she'd never heard of before, and wouldn't be able to find on a map—made famous now only for the protest-turned-riot the previous night, there was a rough, phone-recorded video of three police officers and a young man not much older than Dillon. According to what she'd been hearing so far, the young man, a known lamian protester, had refused to stop when police questioned where he was going. He had a small sign in his hands that read LAMIAN LIVES MATTER, which had been knocked to the ground during the arrest.

The video began with the police asking him where he was going. He stopped immediately and turned around to address them and their question.

That's not how they explained it earlier.

The boy pointed down the street, the subtitles put there by the station claimed he said he was "just going to join my friends in the square for a peaceful protest." He turned to continue on his way.

What happened next was fast, and violent. The taller officer barked something at him. The station did not put his words on the screen and Andrea couldn't quite make it out, but it didn't sound friendly or professional.

The cop to his left roughly grabbed at the boy, while the third took the sign and tossed it.

The first officer then stepped in front of the protestor, angrily gripping the boy's forearm and twisting it around, forcing the frightened youth to spin so the arm was now behind his back. The officer then kicked the back of the boy's leg with his bent knee, forcing him to go down to the ground.

The second cop followed him down, his hand reaching for and making purchase on the scruff of his neck, pushing his face hard into the pavement.

An audible thud was followed by the protestor wailing. "I didn't do nothing!" The video zoomed in on his face. Blood ran freely from his already swelling nose.

The third cop was suddenly in front of the camera. Before a hand blocked the frame and the screen went black, Andrea could see the boy's sign lying against the curb. Broken, like his nose.

"Jesus." She crossed herself. *Did they need to be so rough?*

The video cut away and the camera was now on the anchor again. "The boy is being held for resisting arrest and assaulting a police officer. Several other arrests were made as the protest turned to violence overnight."

Resisting arrest? Andrea wondered how much happened before and after the little bit they showed in the clip. She walked over to the couch and grabbed the remote.

Maybe I should see what the other channels are saying. At least until I have all the locks changed.

THIRTY-SIX

Connor watched the crowd casually stroll, talking in pairs and small groups, as they slowly made their way out of the front door of the Lamplight Foundation's Riverside Manor. The Monday meeting had gone longer than usual and the detective sat in his car, politely waiting for the attendees to leave. After the first few visitors appeared on the front sidewalk, he exited his car and approached the building, stepping off the sidewalk and allowing people to pass him.

"Hey, Dad." Tamara smiled and sped up to give him a hug. "Way to be late."

"Oh no, I'm not here for the meeting. Just to talk to Max."

Tamara slumped her shoulders and rolled her eyes in an over-exaggeration of defeat, "Whyyyyy? Why don't you come with us?"

"This is a you-and-Mom thing. Plus, I can see Max whenever I need. He comes down to the station on a regular basis when we have our sensitivity training or cases or issues that require his help."

"Hi, Mr. Murphy." Madison appeared behind Tamara, both her parents in tow.

Connor nodded to her parents, remembering them as *always polite, but always quiet.* "Glad to see you again, little lady." Connor gave her a broad smile and almost raised his hand up to ruffle her hair, but stopped himself. It had been years since the girls were of an age to appreciate that form of affection. Now it would *mess with their hair.* He looked at the people coming out behind them and back to Tamara. "What? No Brenna?"

"Oh my God, no. She'd never come here. Plus, I don't even know if we'll *ever* see her again. She still hasn't come to school."

"I heard she was transferring." Madison didn't smile when she said it, but Connor heard it in her voice.

"Good riddance." Tamara held a fist up to Madison and the other girl bumped it with her own.

"Connor?" Jacqueline caught up to the group and questioned him with a concerned look.

"Nothing's wrong. I'm just here to talk to Max."

"Oh, Max isn't here." She shook her head. "He left a few minutes ago. But his apprentice, Vic, is inside if you need something."

Connor looked around as if he could see or somehow catch Max before he left but realized he had no idea what the man drove. He chewed his lip and nodded at his wife. "Okay. I'll wait."

"See you at home then?"

"Yeah, I shouldn't be long." Connor kissed her cheek and turned to wink at Tamara. "And if you convince her to stop, tuck a Mint Oreo Blizzard in the freezer for me."

She gave him a thumbs-up and walked away with Madison at her side. He nodded again to Madison's parents and waited for the last few people to exit the building before he pushed the door open and stepped inside.

Closing the heavy oak door behind him, he took a moment to appreciate the ancient wood throughout the foyer and how the gentle light from several well-placed lamps had given the oppressive room a welcoming glow. Seeing no one in the immediate vicinity, he walked toward the parlor he knew was used for the weekly meetings.

He expected to see the man his wife had mentioned, but instead came face-to-face with a young woman in her early to mid-thirties with shockingly pale blonde hair. She was folding chairs and tucking them into a closet large enough to be another room. At the back, the table where he knew refreshments and pamphlets were usually spread out had been cleaned, organized, and put away for another week.

"Excuse me?"

"Yes?" She glanced at him, as she flipped another chair seat up and lifted it to bring to the closet.

"I'm looking for Vic. Well, actually, I'm here for Max but he's gone so I'll talk to Vic until he returns if you could point me toward him."

"I'm Vic." She set the chair down and smiled at him. "Victoria. I'm Max's apprentice. How can I help you?"

"Oh, God. I'm sorry. I shouldn't have assumed." His shame manifested by having him immediately start helping the girl put the chairs away. He quickly folded four, setting them against his leg as he did each, then hooked two in each hand to bring to her. "Here. Sorry. It's nice to see the Council is finally letting women be librarians."

"You know about the Council?" She raised an eyebrow at him.

"Oh, yeah. Sorry again. Jesus I'm apologetic tonight." He almost flushed with embarrassment. *What's wrong with me?* "Detective Connor Murphy—"

"Murphy? Tamara's dad?"

He nodded.

"Oh wait, Connor? *Connor* Murphy? Max's Connor. Oh I never put those two together. That helps make sense of a couple confusing conversations I've had." She laughed at something without filling him in on the joke. "Yeah,

Max is out. Said he needed to go check on something. But he should be back in a bit if you want to wait. If I can help in the meantime, I'll try."

"I wanted to pick his brain about a case." Connor considered what he could have her help him with. "But if you're good with the records, I'd also like to do a search for previous crimes."

"Yeah sure, I can help with that." She pointed at the chairs still sitting behind him. "Help me put these away and I'll make us some coffee."

THIRTY-SEVEN

Henry was beyond disappointed with his searches through the Facebook groups. The only human woman he could find who met the criteria was out of town for the week. She didn't even say where, or for what. His excitement as he was looking over her profile crashed when he saw the post dated the day before, right around the time he'd fallen asleep in the basement. He'd have to wait an entire week if he wanted to grab her.

A week.

It was too long.

The room had been finished by two o'clock Sunday afternoon. He dragged the mattress down two flights of stairs and set it in the enclosed space with a folded sheet and blanket. In the corner next to the floor drain, he put an old metal bait bucket he had found. He pried the spring-loaded lid off and left it open and exposed for his guest to use as a toilet seat. He attached the strong but lightweight chain, found in the grocery store's meager pet department, to the sewer pipe on the wall and adjusted the length.

When he finished, he closed the door and sat down, exhausted, on the mattress. He leaned against the wall and imagined how it would be for her, once he secured his guest. He woke up just after eight-thirty—surprised he'd fallen asleep and a little ashamed to find he was holding himself through his jeans. He wandered upstairs and picked at a microwavable Salisbury steak dinner, glad for the frozen flavorless meal and still shuddering over the previous day's experiments.

The beef liver on Saturday had tasted horrible, even with a thick layer of ketchup on it. He'd only tried it after finishing his pizza because he hated the idea of waste. He quickly wished he hadn't wasted his time cooking it and thrown it away in the first place.

The blood in the container, the reason he'd even purchased the liver in the first place, had been a mistake as well.

For starters, the blood was nothing more than blood-tinted juices and preservatives. Not only did it do nothing for Henry physically, it didn't even clot to appease him mentally.

He couldn't wait a week.

Henry somehow dragged himself through the workday, went home long enough to shower and change, and then drove through the McDonald's for a Double Quarter Pounder meal with a Sprite.

He brought the super-scrubbed and scent-free pickle jar and his ice pick with him out of habit, but they were on the floor on the passenger's side. Not on the seat, ready to use. He wasn't out for blood. He wasn't going to hunt to *kill*, but rather hunt to *catch*. The cops were looking for him. The public was on heightened alert. It was too dangerous. He needed to nab someone quickly and get her into the car, and then into the basement. He wished he had chloroform, but he knew from searching the Internet, he could catch a girl from behind and chokehold her until she passed out. It wouldn't hurt her. It wouldn't hurt the blood.

He parked outside the Lamplight Foundation's weekly meeting, down the street far enough to be out of visual range. Henry watched the building while he ate his heat-lamp meal. He didn't want to grab any of *them*.

They were lamian. He needed a human. But he longed to sit in their meetings and learn their secrets. Unfortunately he couldn't do that. He knew they could read his mind if he got too close. He knew *they* would know his secrets, not just his desires. As the sun went down and it became harder to see anything from that distance, he grew bored and started to drive away.

As he turned at the end of the street and the park came into view, he remembered seeing several of the women online talk about using the park to walk, jog, and otherwise exercise after dinner.

A woman on her own, plugged into her headphones?

It sounded perfect. It reminded Henry of the first one, and the sweet taste of learning what he was missing.

I can't wait a week.

He drove around the park to the other side, where there were several closed businesses and empty parking with no late-day employees wandering about to see him. He pulled into the parking spot in front of a legal office and turned the car off. He took several deep breaths and got out, leaving it unlocked for a easy re-entry once he had someone. Quickly crossing the street, he entered the park through the trees, rather than the pathway.

Crunching through the autumn foliage and rotting underbrush, he made his way to the fountain and benches at the center of the park. He looked around, squinting to study each of the paths meeting in the meager light of the central lampposts.

No one.

"Damn it." He huffed under his breath in the dark and slumped against the tree next to him. Before he could even decide to rethink his location, he heard the rhythmic pattern of a jogger. He smiled and stood up, eager for a view.

The figure came into the light near the fountain, and Henry felt defeated once again. A man. A rather large one at that.

Even with my ice pick, I couldn't take that guy down.

He stepped back deeper into the shadows and realized he may have to be patient.

In less than ten minutes, another set of exercising feet echoed in the distance. This one sounded funny and it took him a minute to realize it was a pair. Exercise buddies whose steps were not quite in sync and therefore made a strange *thump-thump-boom* rhythm as they jogged past him. He hadn't even leaned back against the tree when the unexpected soft padding of a walker came from the path behind him. He turned, gripping hope in his tightened stomach muscles.

It's a girl. Alone.

Henry smiled and watched her approach. As she passed him, he could hear the muffled sounds of the music blaring in her ear buds. *God bless the unaware,* he thought, as he stepped from the shadows of the trees.

Several quick steps and he was on her. She was short, which made it easier, and he reached forward with a wide arc and wrapped a hand around her neck, grabbing his wrist with the other hand and forming the hold that would choke her to unconsciousness.

She squawked, his grip on her neck preventing a full scream, and twisted in his arms. She was tough and fought him, but he was bigger, stronger, and had a firm hold on her.

She clawed backward, trying to find his eyes, then suddenly stopped. She began to wiggle and he realized she might be reaching for a weapon. He braced himself to dodge and whispered, "I won't hurt you. Just stop. *Sleep.*"

The mist from the tiny can in her hand shot an arc over her head, as she pointed it backward and swept from one side to the other.

Henry flinched but didn't dodge well enough, and let out a howl as the contents went directly into the corner of his eye. The burning was immediate, as if his face were on fire, and he pushed her away from him. In the grip of pain, in the anguish of a possible defeat, he pushed her away hard, straight out in front of him. He didn't see her fall. He couldn't see anything with the eye refusing to open, and the other reflexively shut to protect itself.

But he heard the telltale *crack* as she landed against the edge of the fountain.

"Fucking bitch! What the fuck?" He rushed forward, almost tripping over her body, to get to the water in the fountain. He splashed it into his eye and rinsed it the best he could. After several minutes, he raised his head and looked around.

She hadn't run for help. She hadn't gotten up. She lay there where she fell. Blood ran down the side of the short fountain wall and pooled onto the cement below. The injury to her head started right above her eye and wrapped around toward her temple. Her head was split open, but looked like it had been crushed.

It looked almost like the boy's had when Henry hit him with the pipe.

"No." He looked around and felt his pockets. "NO!"

He didn't have a jar to collect the blood spilling from her head. He didn't have his pick to puncture her neck. And he didn't have a living girl to take home and slowly bleed at his leisure.

The blood glistened in the lamplight. The smell rose to meet him.

I'll try again tomorrow. For now—

He bent down and began lapping at the head wound on the fallen girl. He drew his tongue up her cheek, collecting the precious liquid as gravity tried to send it to the cement. He cleaned up the matted hair at her temple like an animal licking her newborn free of placenta. He put his mouth to the crack in her skull. His tongue felt the ridge the fountain wall had created, and he made a slurping sound as he sucked at it.

His heart stopped when she moaned and he pulled back in fear, and confusion.

Alive?

He hadn't checked. He had assumed. Henry looked at the blood on the pavement and realized it wasn't *that* much. The water from the fountain thinning it could make it look like much more than it was.

I can still get her home.

The thought hit him the same time he heard something scrape against cement from somewhere nearby and realized he wasn't alone.

"Fuck." He hissed through his teeth and stood, looking around. His face was smeared with the blood of the girl, from his nose down beyond his chin. He looked like something from a horror movie, something from a nightmare. He licked at his lips and squinted into the darkness around him, trying to locate the sound.

He had his victim. His guest.

His blood supply.

But someone was there. Someone too close, someone who would see him if he tried to carry her, if he was slowed down with her weight.

He growled at the universe, at the unfairness of it all, and ran, leaving her to either bleed to death or be found. *Such a waste.*

He jogged down the path toward his car, going far

enough to be out of the light of the fountain before he slowed to a nervous walk. He didn't want to look guilty if someone passed him. He kept his head down, his bloodied mouth hidden, and followed the twisting path. He listened to the darkness around him. He couldn't *hear* anything.

But he could *feel* someone close by.

Henry's skin tingled and the little hairs on his neck rose. Whoever it was, Henry could feel them getting closer. Coming toward him. He looked around, but couldn't tell which direction to go. He couldn't tell if what he felt was on the path or in the woods, and he froze for a moment, eyes wide enough to feel the cool night air blow across them. It wasn't a squirrel or some other small animals creeping around its nocturnal habitat. This was something else.

This was something that *scared* him.

— THIRTY-EIGHT —

Dillon had slipped out the kitchen door after dinner, escaping the manor to avoid the newbies and curious who would soon be filing in the front for the weekly group session. Even though Madison and Tamara would be there, he still didn't want to be part of the group. Too many people, *lamian*, with powers. His abilities were as fickle as his teen hormones, and nearly impossible to control. He heard things when he didn't want to, he couldn't hear things when he concentrated, and it frustrated him to learn it could take years to control it.

He nodded at the young black couple getting out of their car and sped up his pace before the eager pair tried to talk to him based on his proximity to the property. He crossed the street and headed for the park.

Lying on top of the fountain's umbrellas statue, he stared at the stars and appreciated the quiet. Most people who bothered to come through after dark were wearing headphones and minding their own business. They never even looked up to notice him hidden in the shadows of the only place in the park's center not under the light of lampposts.

Dillon realized he heard the runner's thoughts more easily when they ran past if they were agitated about something—jogging off a fight with their spouse, or listening to their angry exercise music and wishing they had a different job. Other times he heard nothing but the rhythm of their feet on the pavement and maybe muffled music if it was loud enough.

A noise in the brushes behind a bench was loud enough for him to turn his head. He figured it was a squirrel, possibly a night bird, as there wasn't really anything else in the center of town. There had been some excitement a few years back when a bear cub had gotten lost by the river and wandered into town to climb a tree over by the school. But for the most part, nature stuck to the outskirts of town where the road kill was as much a city limits marker as the dinged WELCOME TO RIVERSIDE sign.

A pair of women went by with headphones blaring. *Weird*, he thought. *Exercise partners who don't speak the whole time they're together? Just there to egg the other on?* A few moments later, as he figured the squirrel had scurried off, he watched as a young woman with a brisk stride came from the far path, and the sound in the bushes broke free. The silhouette of a man appeared and walked up behind her, grabbing her roughly around the neck.

Dillon rolled over and went flat on the top of the statue, trying to stay hidden.

What the fuck?

There was a brief struggle as the man tried to choke the woman.

Does he know her? Ex-wife or something?

And then the woman pulled something from her pocket in a tight fist and held it above her head. Dillon heard the sound of something spraying and then the man screamed. The man pushed the woman away from him as he grabbed his face. The woman toppled straight forward—her footing already precarious from the struggle, the shove proved to be more than she could recover from. Momentum and gravity carried her toward the ground and she hit her head hard on the fountain below Dillon. The loud crack sound was enough to make him gasp.

Dillon scooted back and looked through the corner where two umbrellas met, trying to hide from the man. His eyes were wide. He wondered what the hell he should do. His phone was in his pocket, but if he tried to use it right now, the man would hear. He'd get caught. Or worse.

Dillon waited and watched.

The man rinsed his face, swearing under his breath, and Dillon realized she must have used mace on him. *Good for her.* He expected the man to run away, to go back to the shadows or strut off proud of himself.

He was *not* expecting the man to lean down and start licking the blood off the woman's face.

Dillon froze. His thoughts swirled and mixed, fear and anger, lust and hunger.

Wait. Dillon shook his head. They weren't *his* thoughts, but rather those of the man below him. The man who was mad she had fought back, and angry she died. The man who wanted to drink all her blood, but didn't have a jar with him.

A jar?

Dillon sat back a little, wishing he were out of range of the man's thoughts.

The man was already planning to go out the *next* night. He would take his ice pick. He would—

Oh my God, this is the guy. The guy from TV.

Dillon realized he was watching the man who had murdered several people in town, including the kids from his school and this poor woman lying on the cement below him. Dillon tried to carefully climb down the backside of the statue. He needed to slip into the trees and vanish before this guy saw him.

And then the woman moaned and both the man below and Dillon jumped in reaction to it, Dillon's foot slid against the statue and made a strange scraping noise. The man stopped and looked around.

Did he hear my shoe? Shit.

Dillon stood still on the backside of the statue, balancing on the edge of the statue above the water, effectively blocked from the view of the man. He held his breath and waited.

The man didn't appear on either side of the statue. He didn't step around the fountain searching for the source of the sound.

For fear of making further noise, Dillon held his breath and slipped down, stepping into the water, rather than leaping from the statue to the short wall like he normally would. He counted to three to allow for a reaction from the man. When there was none, Dillon turned and quietly slid his feet through the shallow fountain away from the statue in its center. He stepped out and exhaled slowly. He crouched low and remained still for another few moments, letting the water pool at his feet to avoid his now-soaked shoes from sloshing when he moved. He stood and took several careful steps to test his sneakers. Satisfied he could sneak away, he walked as fast as he could down the path toward the manor, keeping the fountain and large statue, between him and the man.

He could hear the man's thoughts continue behind him. Could hear him contemplating taking the woman home, but then the man heard something.

Yeah, me, ya dummy.

The man changed his mind and reluctantly left her there, sprawled at the base of the fountain. He sprinted down the path toward the small offices on Second Street. As the man's fading thoughts moved out of range, Dillon heard him suddenly worry about something the man could sense but not see. Something that scared him enough for Dillon to pause and worry for a moment.

Dillon couldn't hear any other thoughts but the man's.

Bah, it's just me. Keep running, fucker.

Dillon looked over his shoulder at the other path, hoping the man was still going the other direction and hadn't doubled-back. When he turned around to continue toward the manor, he almost ran straight into Maximilian, who was walking very briskly down the park pathway.

"Max." Dillon looked up but said nothing more. The look on Max's face told him he didn't need to. He was scanning the woods and the path beyond Dillon. Dillon presumed the old lamian had likely been listening since he had entered the park half a block back.

"Call the police." Max walked past Dillon without slowing down and headed straight for the center of the park.

Dillon watched him walk around the fountain, out of sight, and wondered how Max would react to the sight of the woman lying there. Dillon pulled his phone from his pocket, turned back to the path out of the park, and dialed 911.

THIRTY-NINE

Connor's phone vibrated in his pocket and he excused himself from the conversation with Victoria to answer it. The screen said DESK.

"Where the fuck are you, Murphy? You still over at Lamplight?"

"Yeah, why?"

"Get your ass to the park. Some kid just called. Said a man killed a girl by the fountain, and—and I'm not making this shit up—he *heard him thinking* about all the other murders."

"What?"

"Kid said the perp was heading toward Second Street. I'm sending squads."

"I'm on it." Connor hung up, shoved his phone in his pocket, and stood.

Heading straight for the front door and pulling his gun as he did, he turned back to Victoria. "Lock this door." He was out and across the street before the deadbolt slammed into place.

The park was quiet, and mostly dark. The street lamps were decorative at best, and only hinted at safety in ten-foot circles of sickly yellow spaced far enough apart to offer more than enough shadows. Even that meager light was only along the paths and left the wooded areas under whatever dim light the moon offered. He glanced up at the moonless sky and quickly assessed his options. He chose to avoid the park altogether, instead running straight down the outer edge of the trees, along the sidewalk where regular streetlights provided better lighting.

The length of two blocks wasn't far, but as a detective rather than street cop, he didn't run often, and he felt the burn almost immediately. The idea his killer was *right there* kept the pain from actually affecting him.

Connor arrived at the other end of the park and stopped. Holding his department-issued Beretta out in front of him, he surveyed the street's closed businesses, sidewalks, and smattering of half a dozen vehicles. One of the cars had an open door and he approached it quickly, quietly, his .40 out in front of him the entire time.

As he drew closer, the shadows separated from the darkness and he saw the crumpled form of a man lying next to the car. Connor squatted and looked around. There was no other motion in the immediate vicinity. He reached down to slip his hand around the man's throat and feel for a pulse, but his fingers found the warmth of fresh blood and exposed tissue as they slid right into an open wound. He turned the man over by a shoulder and gasped.

Pulling his flashlight from his pocket with his clean hand, Connor shined it on the man and jumped back, revolted. Blood was smeared and beginning to dry all over the man's mouth and down his chin, as if he'd been in a pie-eating contest and had buried his face in the blueberry filling. Below that, the man's throat had been torn out. Not a puncture, or even several, which were then torn. Not a desperate clawing of the surface tissue. The flesh had been dug into for purchase and peeled away, left hanging like an open door, exposing his trachea, muscles and cords to the night air. The white of several vertebrae poking out from behind the gore. The man's blood coated the front of his shirt and had pooled on the pavement where he'd laid. Connor gagged, knowing what he had felt when checking for a pulse hadn't been the smears on the dead man's face, but rather the viscera of his destroyed neck.

Connor wiped his bloodied hand on his pants and scanned the scene with his flashlight. The open car door was washed with great sprays of bloody wetness and clinging bits of meat, letting him know the man had been crouching—likely begging for his life—when his throat had been shredded. The interior of the vehicle was speckled in blood drops, peripheral and accidental from the direction of the attack and likely happened when the man spun to land facedown. The splatter glistened against the dark interior of the car as if sequins had been spilled across the seat and steering wheel.

Connor swallowed back bile in response to the ferocious mess in front of him, and aimed the flashlight across the other cars and dark windows of the street, surveying the area for any movement. The local businesses were closed. There were no restaurants or convenience stores on this side of the park to provide nighttime services. There was *usually* no nightlife on Second Street other than those heading into or out of the park. Tonight was no different.

He stood and shined his light further into the open vehicle, careful not to touch the door or smear the blood. The interior of the car was mostly tidy, other than a McDonald's bag on the passenger side floor fresh enough Connor could still smell the fries it had recently held. There was a soda in the console cup holder, a pair of sunglasses in the cubby below the stereo, and a dried-up air freshener sticking out of the plastic air vent slats. He leaned in carefully, ignoring the smell of the splattered gore in the small space, and used his flashlight to move the fast-food bag. He pulled back as his light hit the floor mat and its contents.

"Son of a bitch." An ice pick lay on the floor, reflecting the beam of the flashlight back to him. A wooden handled, eight-inch, cheap looking ice pick. Connor looked from the weapon to the man's bloodied face.

What the fuck?

If you're the guy, then who—

He bent down and looked at the body again. The blood around the man's mouth wasn't from the neck wound. It was separate. And it made Connor question, *lamian?*

He pulled a pen from his pocket and lifted the man's lip, looking for a bloodstained tongue or teeth to back up his hunch. He raised his eyebrows at the empty sockets where the canines should have been. The inside of the man's mouth wasn't coated with only the blood he *may* have been drinking, but with the blood still oozing from the damaged gums where his teeth had been ripped free.

Of course, if the teeth had been there, he knew he wouldn't have known by sight alone if the man had been human or lamian. But his job had taught him they were both capable of horrible things, *both* could be dangerous in the wrong circumstances, and curiosity under the guise of police instincts had never lead him astray.

But you can't tell evil from its dental imprint alone.

The tiny hairs on the back of Connor's neck started to tickle, and he suddenly felt uncomfortable. He wasn't alone out here and he knew it. He could sense it. The prickling crept down his spine and he started to slowly look around the front of the car at the businesses on his side of the street, keeping the speed of his movements to a minimum and making as little noise as possible.

"I suggest you shoot him now and reduce your paperwork."

Connor stood up and spun around, his Beretta out in front of him. Crossing the street, Max casually stuffed a handkerchief into the inner breast pocket of his suit jacket.

"Jesus, Max. What the fuck? I could have *shot* you."

"Wouldn't be the first time a cop shot me." Max proffered a weak half-smile as he closed the gap between them.

Connor wasn't sure if it was a joke or a source of contention, a sore spot he didn't know the man carried. He watched, as the elderly lamian approached the body and looked down with no more emotion than a scientist examining a petri dish of bacteria.

"That's your murderer." He nodded at the man on the ground and looked back to Connor. "The boy staying with us saw him in the park, saw him kill the girl there. That man matches the exact description running around the boy's thoughts. There was a familiarity he couldn't quite place, but I'm sure once he calms down he'll be more helpful."

"I thought you didn't do that?"

"Do *what*?" Max furrowed his brows at Connor.

"Go digging inside minds."

Max's tense expression relaxed. "We do when it's necessary. Humans don't like us to on the street, but boy do they *love* our help when it suits them."

Connor cocked his head at Max, not understanding the current attitude of the normally proper, if not uptight and restrained, lamian. Max seemed *off*, and Connor figured it was likely a reaction to the dead body on the ground. *I wonder if the smell of blood does something to them?*

"What did you mean, *shoot him*? Why would I do that? He's dead. Look at his throat. Something horribly violent and crazy happened here."

Max nodded, "Yes, and I've seen this before, Connor."

"Before? When?"

"A *very* long time ago. Almost a hundred years now." Max's gaze drifted for a moment. "Throat torn out. Were the teeth taken?"

Connor nodded. The sound of sirens in the distance let him know the cavalry was on its way.

"The same as back then." Max chewed on his lip, as he considered his words.

"Did they catch the guy? You think he was lamian, served time and is out now? I'm switching one murderer for another?"

Max shook his head, his calm almost contagious. "No, they never caught him. Never stood a chance. And it's not like that. It's…" Max focused on Connor's face and spoke without blinking. "I can assure you, it's done. It's not a *new* case to worry about. It's over. *All* of it."

"Done? Just like that?"

"Yes, Connor. This *human* was playing a game, longing to become one of *us*. And one of us stepped in and stopped him."

Connor heard contempt in Max's voice and for the briefest moment pondered if it were for humankind, or especially for this particular specimen. Max looked at the body with enough visible disgust Connor thought he might spit on the corpse.

"Your murderer? This guy? He wasn't taken out by another *killer*, but by a *cleaner*. One who won't likely strike again. Not here. Not in *your* lifetime."

Max looked up from the body on the ground and implored Connor with his eyes as much as his words. "You go ahead now and shoot him in the neck near the wound there. Put some gunpowder on *your* hand and *his* flesh. And then *you* take credit for stopping him. Otherwise your chief, your mayor, your citizens, they're all going to have you chasing a ghost you'll *never* see again. Let alone catch. Better to be done with it." He paused and softened his voice. "Close the cases, Connor. Move on."

Connor looked at Max and contemplated his words. He'd known the lamian since he'd first joined the force almost twenty years ago. He had no reason *not* to trust him, *not* to believe him. He looked around the empty street, squinting his eyes toward the darkness of the park. He didn't feel anyone watching anymore, didn't sense anyone nearby. There was no one out here now but him and Max. And Max seemed comfortable, and sure of his words.

He's been around a long time. He's seen a lot. If this is an old M.O., I can find it in the files and prove it to the chief.

"No files go back that far, Connor." Max looked down the road toward the sound of sirens getting louder. "You don't have a lot of time here. Trust me."

Connor looked at Max's eyes and saw certainty. A confidence he didn't want to question, as he suddenly didn't think he wanted to know the reasoning behind it. He *knew* this was his killer lying on the ground. The ice pick. The witness. And he knew he trusted Max.

"This isn't going to bite me in the ass?"

"Why would it? You're the hero. Stopped the killer." Max nodded at the car. "His weapon is right there. His DNA is *all over* the crime scene back there." He looked sideways, indicating the park.

"There's a body by the fountain?" Connor asked, cementing his decision in the back of his mind. *Victim number seven. It took seven people before this guy was stopped. And although the authorities didn't stop him, he* was *stopped.*

"Yes, a young woman. She almost survived." Max shook his head, his face full of reverence. "Almost."

"Can you head back that way for me? Keep the joggers at bay until the boys in blue get there. I'll come to the house for a statement from you and your ward." Connor turned back to the body on the ground and sighed loudly. "After I take care of this."

"Absolutely, Detective." Max sounded reverent, almost subservient as he lowered his head. He turned away from Connor, his mouth thinning to a resolute smile.

Max didn't flinch when the single gunshot went off behind him, but he turned back to Connor. The detective had squatted low to line up the shot. Feeling the gaze from across the street, Connor turned to face Max as he stood and exhaled through his mouth in an exaggeration of effort.

Done.

Connor was sure he was covering something. But he was also confident in Max's assessment that it was over. The men nodded to each other, silently agreeing to keep the bullet's mission a secret. Max turned and entered the dimly lit park.

The sound of sirens filled the street, as several squads turned the far corner and finally came into view. Connor walked to the rear of the killer's car to wait for his unit to get to work on the scene.

He glanced back at the body on the ground and frowned at the destruction of the man's throat. He thought about the damage he'd seen before his bullet had made it worse, made it unrecognizable. He had many questions about who had done it. Many questions he'd never be able to ask on the record.

Connor shook them free, unable to hear his own thoughts over the sirens as they approached. He made a motion with his hand in front of his throat for the officers to cut the noise, and his ears rang for a few moments afterward.

Across the street, Maximilian had shoved his hands into his pockets and was taking long strides, as he headed toward the fountain and the dead woman lying there. The sirens had stopped wailing behind him, and the woods and paths around him seemed deserted. In the silence of the park, the only sound was the freshly harvested human teeth, clicking against each other in his pocket.

— ABOUT THE AUTHOR —

Born and raised in Wisconsin, Kelli Owen now lives in Pennsylvania. She's attended countless writing conventions, participated on dozens of panels, and spoken at the CIA Headquarters in Langley, VA. Visit her website at kelliowen. com for more information. F/F

99522078R00137

Made in the USA
Columbia, SC
13 July 2018